BRIDE FOR EASTON

Mail Order Mounties: Alberta

CASSIE HAYES

RNWMP: Bride for Easton

Copyright © 2017 by Cassie Hayes

All rights reserved. No part of this book may be reproduced in any form by any electronic or mechanical means including photocopying, recording, or information storage and retrieval without permission in writing from the author.

ISBN 978-1979452755

www.CassieHayes.com

Cover design by EDH Graphics
Edited by Jessica Valliere

First Edition
Printed in the USA

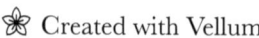 Created with Vellum

CHAPTER 1

It was the prettiest bedroom Molly Hennessy had ever laid eyes on. Instead of stark white walls and drab beige curtains, this room welcomed her like as if she were its long-lost princess.

Pale pink flowers popped off the cream wallpaper like miniature bouquets picked just for her, and the matching pink draperies begged to be stroked. Before she even knew she'd reached out to do just that, Molly gasped and jerked back her hand as if the fabric was as hot as molten lava.

"This *isn't* your room," she whispered to herself as she set her small leather suitcase on the bed. It sank into the soft down comforter, tempting Molly to hop up on the full-size bed and revel in the luxury. Before she could decide whether allowing herself the pleasure would be a sin, a knock sounded on her half-closed door.

Spinning around, her cheeks flaming with embarrassment at almost being caught, she smiled at the two young women who poked their heads into her room. *Not your room!*

"You must be Molly," said the taller of the two. "I'm Claire Anderson…soon to be Claire Clark."

"And I'm Beth," said the other.

"Nice to meet you," Molly said, reaching out to give them both firm handshakes. They appeared bemused, but Molly barely noticed. She was more curious about what had brought these two pretty ladies to Miss Hazel's. "Isn't there one more of us?"

"Yes, that would be Sinead. She's around somewhere. Did you know she's a doctor? A real life, trained *doctor!*"

Molly did not, in fact, know that, but her surprise quickly turned to excitement. They would have so much to talk about. "Really? I can't wait to meet her."

"Miss Hazel asked us to find you. Our first lesson will start in ten minutes."

"Oh, then I'd better go fetch my shawl. I set it out by the fire downstairs to dry. Thank goodness I got here before it started raining in earnest."

"If you see Sinead down there, will you remind her about our lesson?" Claire called as Molly hurried down the hallway.

"Sure!"

Molly would have loved to stay and chat with her new friends, but she couldn't risk losing her shawl. She would lay it out on her big bed before the lessons started and it would be dry by the time she made it back to her room.

As she entered the main sitting room, where she'd left the shawl draped across the back of a chair near the fireplace, Molly stopped short. Whatever happy or hopeful feelings that had been trying to take root in her heart withered at the scene before her.

A woman she didn't know, but guessed was Sinead, stood in front of a big mirror with Molly's shawl draped around her shoulders, admiring her own reflection. Even in her surprise, Molly had to admit it was a reflection that deserved to be admired. The woman was much taller than Molly, and she had fine features and silky bronze skin that was complimented by the shawl's rich gold and red hues. But almost before the thought flitted through her mind, a blinding red rage clouded her vision.

"That's mine!" she shouted, doing her best to shoot flaming arrows of anger from her eyes.

The woman spun around, her eyes wide and her full lips forming a perfect O. "I-I'm so s-sorry," she stammered, pulling the shawl from her shoulders and holding it out in front of her as if it might be contaminated with cholera germs or something. "I wasn't going to take it, I just wanted to see what it would look like. I'm so, so sorry."

Within the span of a single blink, Molly's rage drained away, leaving her slightly embarrassed.

"It's okay," she said, crossing the room to take the scarf. Even though she'd already forgiven the woman, Molly still clutched the fabric against her thumping chest. If she'd lost it… "I grew up in a big family, so I'm overly protective of my things. I'm Molly, by the way."

"My name's Sinead," the other woman said with a tentative smile, taking Molly's proffered hand.

Any tension that might have lingered between them blew away in a puff. "I really need to work on my temper," Molly admitted, her cheeks heating up. "Everyone tells me it's going to get me in trouble one day."

Sinead's laugh reminded Molly of a crackling

fire on a cold day. "I don't blame you. It's stunning. Did you knit it?"

Molly's left eyelid twitched, and she dropped her gaze as she caressed the soft material. "No, my mother did. She gave it to me the day I left for the convent."

Tense silence stretched between them for a moment, before Sinead broke it by changing the subject. "So Miss Hazel tells me you're a midwife."

Dragging herself out of her maudlin mood, Molly smiled. "Yes. And you're a doctor, I hear."

"That's right," Sinead said, lifting her head slightly, almost as if too many people had questioned her on her occupation. "But I don't have that much experience with birthing babies. It's a relief to know you'll be there, just in case."

Molly honestly hadn't thought about using her skills in her new home. "Isn't it just some small health resort for the wealthy? How many babies could possibly be born there?"

Sinead gave her a wink. "People are people, Molly, no matter where they are or how much money they have."

Molly blushed at the unspoken insinuation. She'd spent her life specifically *not* thinking about how babies were made, instead focusing on bringing them into the world.

"I hope you're right, Sinead. Oh, I'm supposed to tell you our first lesson starts in a few minutes."

"Good! Maybe we could go in early and you could show me around the kitchen. I'm afraid my schooling interfered with learning domestic duties."

"Um…" Molly hesitated, unsure about leaving her beloved shawl behind, but decided to stop being silly. "Sure," she finally said, draping it across the chair again. At least it would be fully dry *and* toasty warm later.

As Molly gave Sinead a tour of the kitchen — it was pretty much the same as any other kitchen — she felt a bond growing between them. Sinead probably came from a wealthy family, or at least a family better off than Molly's, and she was far more educated, yet she didn't put on airs. She was quick to smile, and long before Miss Hazel came bustling into the kitchen, they'd locked arms and were giggling like sisters.

"I see my two doctors have met already," the older woman said, grinning at them each in turn.

Molly laughed. "I'm not a doctor, Miss Hazel. Just a midwife."

Miss Hazel snorted her opinion on that. "Nonsense! Don't forget, I've given birth, my dear. I know precisely what goes on, and let me tell you, I would rather have had my midwife over scraggy old Dr. Westheyemer. No offense, Sinead."

"None taken," Sinead said. "I agree wholeheartedly."

Molly's cheeks flamed from the compliments. Yes, she'd worked hard during her training, and she honestly loved it — but her motivations for becoming a midwife had been less than selfless. She hardly deserved their praise. Besides, flattery felt unnatural to her.

Perhaps sensing Molly's discomfort, Miss Hazel deftly changed the subject. "Are you both ready to learn how to properly care for your future husbands? I have so much in store for you, you'll probably wish you were back in medical school!"

Molly bit her tongue to stop herself from pointing out midwives didn't go to medical school. She didn't want to get the praise train rolling again.

"I have so much to learn," Sinead said with a sigh.

Molly snaked her arm around her new friend's waist. "But I'm going to help you along the way. I grew up the oldest of fifteen children, so I know a thing or two about keeping a home."

"I just hope Matthew is patient with me."

Molly's eyes narrowed in warning. "If he isn't, he'll have to answer to me!"

Miss Hazel cackled in delight. "Oh, Easton is going to have his hands full with you, my dear. If you ask me, you're exactly what a man like him needs."

Molly wasn't sure how to take that. Her future husband's sole letter to her had been short and to the point, with no real romance in it at all. That hadn't particularly bothered her, but it had left her wondering what he was like. It didn't really matter, but she'd prayed for a man who might eventually love her.

"That reminds me," Miss Hazel said, pulling something from the bodice of her dress. "This came for you a few minutes ago."

Miss Hazel held out an envelope, and all Molly could do was stare at it. Her heart sped up to double-time, and she found it difficult to breathe.

"Molly?" Sinead's voice echoed as if down a long hallway as Molly willed her hand to move.

"T-thank you," she finally managed, taking the envelope and turning it over. As soon as she saw the familiar, loopy script, her heart sank. "Excuse me."

She hurried out of the kitchen and tore open

the letter in the privacy of the hallway.

Dearest Molly,

How strange it is to call you that! After so many years, I am afraid you will always be Mary Theresa in my heart, but I am profoundly happy you have found your true path in life.

The sisters have asked me to relate their well-wishes in your upcoming adventures. We all miss your energy, as well as your lovely soprano. Sister Agnes has yet to find a replacement for you in the choir.

You may be feeling anxious, or even frightened about what may lay ahead, but I would counsel you to have faith in the Lord. He has a plan for you; and as you have discovered, we mere mortals are powerless to work against that plan. Remember Joshua 1:9 to comfort you during the uncertain times ahead.

> *Have not I commanded thee? Be strong and of a good courage; be not afraid, neither be thou dismayed, for the Lord thy God is with thee whithersoever thou goest.*

I am sorry to report that your mother has yet to reply to my request for an audience, but there again, have faith! She is a good woman who loves you deeply. I know she will not forsake you in the end.

Be well, Mary Theresa, and please write to us about all your adventures in Alberta. With your enthusiastic spirit and caring nature, I know your husband will forgive your occasional fits of pique, though I would advise you to continue your work on that particular trait.

Grace and blessings on your path, Reverend Mother Perpetua Louise Convent of the Sisters of Redemption

Molly scrubbed the tears from her cheeks, tucked the letter in the pocket of her drab woolen skirt, and swallowed hard. Mother Superior's belief in Molly warmed her heart, but not enough to burn away the cold left by her own mother's rejection. That kind of pain would never fade.

※

EASTON COOPER STEPPED through the door of the Cougar Springs Mountie station fifteen minutes before he was scheduled for duty, as usual. Nathaniel Clark and Samuel Murray were collecting their things as they prepared to leave for the day.

"Afternoon, sir," Nathaniel said, shooting a glance at the clock to confirm the time.

"Anything to report?" Easton asked, waiting patiently by the door for Samuel to vacate their shared desk.

Samuel shook his head. "All quiet, sir. The only

thing that caught my eye on my noon patrol was ol' Ezekiel heading into Sam's. And I don't think he was stopping for lunch."

Easton frowned. "Starting early today."

"The old fool's going to drink himself into an early grave if he isn't careful," Nathaniel said with a sad shake of his head.

They'd been saying the same thing about Ezekiel Chambers ever since he stumbled into Cougar Springs four years earlier, and the man didn't look a day older than when he arrived. He claimed to have struck it rich in the gold rush, but always avoided saying which one. Judging by his leathery skin, scraggy mop of grey hair, and cloudy eyes, it was certainly possible he meant the San Francisco rush, but Easton wasn't the type of man who liked to guess about such trivial things. If it didn't matter to his job, it didn't matter to him.

"I'll start my rounds as soon as Matthew gets here," Easton said, hanging his hat on his hook so the strap was centered and the front crease pointed perfectly straight up and down.

"That would be now, boss." Matthew strolled through the door and flopped into the chair Nathaniel had just barely vacated. "But don't you want to move that inkwell back where it belongs?"

Easton narrowed his eyes at the grinning Mountie. Everyone knew Easton liked things just so, but he rarely imposed his quirks on the men who served under him. Instead of asking Samuel to not move anything on their shared desk, Easton simply came in early every day to arrange things to his liking. What was the harm in that?

Of course, once Matthew mentioned the inkwell, Easton's eyes could barely stop from seeking it out. As he stared down the younger man, he could see from the corner of his eye that the inkwell sat precariously close to the edge of the desk, all the way on the left side, instead of the right, where it belonged. His skin itched at the thought of someone knocking it over and making a mess, but he wasn't about to show any weakness in front of his men.

Only once Samuel and Nathaniel had finally left for the day did he sit and quietly arrange his space, saving the inkwell for last. Just as he set it down and started reading the forecast that had come in overnight, a young man burst into the office.

"Fight at Sam's!" His eyes were wild and excited. "Fight at the saloon!" With that, he spun on his heel and tore off back toward Sam's, no doubt to watch the fracas.

"What now?" Matthew groaned as he shoved his hat down around his ears.

"Probably just Ezekiel mouthing off," Easton said, followed by a deep sigh as he stood to fetch his hat.

Instead of cramming it on his head, he fitted it so it sat level on his head, as he'd been trained to do. No sloppy technique for him, even if it took a few moments longer.

"C'mon, boss, there's trouble brewing down at the O.K. Corral!"

Easton chuckled. "Let's hope it's not of the same variety."

Matthew seemed antsy to run down to Sam's, but Easton never ran if it could be helped. Running evoked a sense of panic, something a Mountie should never show, even if he felt it. Communities looked to Mounties for guidance, so it was of paramount importance for them to remain calm at all times and exude nothing but confidence. A brisk stride evoked that sense of strong urgency, and was nearly as fast as a sprint, while maintaining the dignity of the uniform.

Easton had to put his shoulder into Sam's heavy wooden door to get it open, then he was hit with a hot wall of stink. Cigar smoke mixed with the vapor from whatever alcohol Sam had on special today, then it all coagulated with the ripe odor of more than a decade's worth of men reveling inside. Sometimes the stench was so strong, he barely had the stomach to stay any longer than it took to wolf down his daily supper.

A quick scan of the room told him Ezekiel was the only threat, if the old sot could be called that. Stepping into the close room, Easton watched the man as he staggered toward a middle-aged fellow who sat at a nearby table, enjoying one of Sam's famous steak dinners.

"You think you're better'n me!" Ezekiel slurred, his eyelids drooping heavily. "Huh? You do, dontchya?"

The poor man appeared startled, then shifted his gaze away from Ezekiel, no doubt hoping he'd be left in peace if he ignored the drunk. No such luck. Ezekiel slammed his hands on the man's table, making the plate — and the man — jump several inches.

"Enough of that, now," Easton said quietly, but with authority. He'd found it to be far more effective than shouting.

Every living thing in the saloon froze, including Sam's pet monkey, ChiChi. Every eye turned to the commander of the Mounties, who had a reputation for not tolerating nonsense. Ezekiel managed to pull himself upright and hung his head in shame. Without a word, he sulked over to Easton and mumbled something that sounded like an apology.

"Matthew, please escort Mr. Chambers back to the office so he can sleep it off," Easton said, taking off his hat. "I'm going to grab a bite before I start my rounds."

"Surprise, surprise," Matthew teased as he collected Ezekiel and headed back to the office.

The moment the door closed against the brisk wind blowing, the familiar sounds of Sam's Saloon resumed. Glasses clinked on the hardwood bar, men chatted and more than occasionally laughed, and ChiChi squeaked and chittered as she swung from the top of the bar mirror to a light fixture to an ornately carved cornice. She finally settled on the broad head of a stuffed grizzly bear hanging from the wall.

Easton had barely settled in at his regular table when someone approached.

"What a way to start your shift, eh Commander?"

Sam Bonney, the owner of the only saloon in Cougar Springs, settled across from him and smiled.

Every day, Easton wondered what had led Sam to own a bar, and every day he was grateful for that decision. He'd never met a more contentious, down-to-earth, and caring saloon owner.

"Is that a new dress, Sam?" he asked. "Color suits you."

Sam made a show of blushing like a much younger woman, and smoothed her hands down the sides of her green silk dress. "This old thing? Actually, one of the maids at the hotel made it for me. I think she has a promising future as a seamstress, don't you?"

Easton didn't know about such things, but he agreed just the same.

"Would you like to try today's special, Commander? A fragrant beef Burgundy with roasted winter vegetables."

"No thanks, Sam. Just my usual."

Sam chuckled and went to fetch his order. He couldn't understand why she always tried to serve him some of her cook's fancy food, when all he ever wanted was steak and potatoes. But she never failed to ask, which was the sign of a smart entrepreneur, as far as he was concerned.

Before he could even wonder where his lunch was, Sam set a loaded plate in front of him. As was his habit, he breathed in the scent of the rare steak and steaming baked potato, topped with a hunk of butter the size of a walnut. He smirked at the pile of Brussels sprouts nestled next to the steak. She knew he wouldn't eat them, but she never failed to put *something* green on his plate.

As he tucked in, Sam leaned forward. "So I hear I'm going to be losing your business very soon."

Easton frowned as he chewed, wondering what she was going on about. "Huh?"

It was Sam's turn to frown. "Well, your new wife will no doubt want to show off her cooking skills to her groom, don't you think?"

Honestly, he'd never thought about it one way or the other. In fact, he'd spent the last few weeks doing his level best to *not* think about his bride at all. Every time he found his mind wandering toward what she might be like, he stopped himself and thought of something else. What he really wanted was a woman who could keep herself occupied — not hard to do in Cougar Springs — and leave him alone.

"Hmm…" he mused, then stuffed another hunk of meat in his mouth so he wouldn't have to speak.

"Besides," she added, leaning back as she

watched him closely, "most brides aren't keen on their new husbands preferring to spend time in a saloon instead of with them."

Understanding dawned on him. He froze mid-chew and met Sam's dancing eyes. She burst out laughing, clapping her hands in delight at his discomfort.

"Oh honey, *everything* is going to be different as soon as she arrives," she said as she stood to get back to her duties. "Where you eat your meals is the least of your worries."

Panic flared in Easton's chest. It wasn't a sensation he was used to, and to hide his distress he started rearranging everything on the table. His mind raced as he slid the salt and pepper shakers to the midpoint between the edge of his plate and the edge of the table. He wondered exactly what he'd gotten himself into as he used his knife to push the food into segregated piles. He fretted over how the whole crazy scheme would work out as he folded his napkin over and over until Sam laid her hand on his, stilling him.

"Easton, honey," she said quietly, so no one else could hear. "Sometimes change is a good thing."

Easton watched her walk away and didn't believe a word she said.

CHAPTER 2

"I'm so nervous, Molly," Sinead murmured as they peered out the window at the picturesque scene whizzing past.

Molly turned to her friend — her *best* friend — and scowled. "About what? Matthew is the luckiest man alive, if you ask me. Don't tell the others, but you're the best of us, Sinead."

Sinead opened her mouth to object, but Molly stopped. "Don't even try to pretend otherwise. We all know it, and it doesn't bother us a bit. You're beautiful, you're smart, you're kind, *and* you're a doctor. What more could a mail-order husband ask for?"

Sinead pressed her lips into a thin line and said nothing, but Molly knew what worried her friend. Molly may have spent most of her life training to become a nun, but she wasn't so sheltered that she didn't understand Sinead's skin color had been an issue with ignorant bigots in the past…and might in the future.

Molly wrapped her fingers around Sinead's cool hand and squeezed. "We're all here for you, and we all love you, come what may. Understand?"

Sinead's dark eyes met Molly's, and they shared a moment of unadulterated sisterly love. When wetness began pooling in Sinead's eyes, Molly sniffed and grinned. "Nope. None of that. Look, there's the station up ahead."

The train lurched and screeched as it came to a stop in the most beautiful town Molly had ever seen, not that she'd seen much outside Ottawa. It might have been a page cut from a magazine advertisement for Cougar Springs Health Institute. Mountains ringed the small community, which was dominated by what looked almost like a castle a short distance away — no doubt the famed sanitarium itself.

When Miss Hazel had informed the four brides they were heading for a "sanitarium," Molly had nearly bolted out of the door, but Miss Hazel had been quick to explain it wasn't an insane asylum, as Molly had feared, but rather a sort of luxury hotel where the wealthy sought treatments for all sorts of ailments, from arthritis to cancer. Rumor had it the hot springs the Institute was built around carried miraculous healing waters. Molly didn't believe it. Neither did Sinead, which strengthened the bond between them.

"There they are!" Claire cried, pointing at a group of tall men in red uniforms standing in a perfect line in the middle of the platform.

The one standing a few inches in front of the rest caught Molly's attention. Everything about him looked precise, from the way his hat sat level on his head to the way his polished boots were clamped together in a model 'at attention' pose. He could have stepped right out of a Royal North West Mounties recruitment poster. He had to be the commander of the others, which meant he was Easton Cooper, which meant he was her future husband.

"Oh my…" she breathed.

"Ooh, that one must be yours, Molly," Beth said from the next row. "He's very handsome."

Molly barely heard her for the pulse pounding in her ears. Tears prickled at the back of her eyes as she sent up a little prayer of gratitude. Maybe God wasn't angry with her for leaving the order after all.

During all the hours of lessons at Miss Hazel's, and then the long train ride, Molly imagined God would punish her by matching her with an ugly old man who treated her poorly. She had no idea if Easton was kind, but she'd been wrong on the first two counts, so hopefully she'd be wrong on the last.

"It'd serve me right if I wasn't wrong," she mumbled to herself, the darkness of self-loathing looming over her.

"What was that, dear?" Miss Hazel asked as she pulled a bag from the overhead rack.

"Nothing," Molly said, jumping up and following suit. Of course, unlike the others, the small case she pulled down was her *only* bag, but that would just make unpacking quicker.

"Ladies!" Miss Hazel called, while the rest of the passengers disembarked. "Follow me to your new lives!"

Molly was first bride to step off the train, and she shifted from one foot to the other while Miss Hazel approached the Mounties. Excitement overpowered self-doubt, leaving her itching to meet her groom. The man she knew in her heart was Easton removed his hat in one elegant motion and held it to his stomach, then kissed Miss Hazel's hand.

"Oh, you're quite the charmer," Miss Hazel

said, giggling like a schoolgirl. "Molly! Molly Hennessy!"

Yes! She'd been right.

Shaking her red hair back, Molly squared her shoulders and strode forward. She found it hard to stop grinning like an idiot, then decided it didn't matter. If Easton didn't like a woman who smiled, the man was going to have a very hard life.

Grabbing his hand in a firm handshake, she said, "Hi! I'm Molly Hennessy. You must be Easton Cooper. I believe I'm supposed to be your bride. Nice to meet you!"

Easton blinked as if he was taken aback by something, though she couldn't imagine what. Then that stern façade dropped across his eyes again, and he pulled her hand to his lips.

"Pleasure to meet you, Miss Hennessy," he said, just before his lips grazed the back of her hand.

A firestorm started at the point of contact and swept up Molly's arm, straight to her cheeks. Being fair-skinned, she always had blushed easily, but this felt so much hotter than even her worst blush. Worse yet, she liked it.

A lot.

Without another word, Easton took her case, then wrapped her blazing hand into the crook of his arm and led her to the steps. Pausing at each, he made sure she didn't trip or stumble, then marched off into the crowd bustling around them.

Molly had never been left speechless in her life, but she'd never met anyone like Easton before either. Of course, she hadn't had much of a chance to at the convent. She dared to peek up at him as they strode toward a small church just down the street from the train station, no doubt where they would marry. He stood no less than a foot taller than her, and his muscular frame spoke of long hours of hard work. His black hair had been cropped short, and his tanned neck hinted that he never let it grow much longer. The sun shimmering in his deep blue eyes reminded her of a summer afternoon at a cold, deep lake.

'Handsome' didn't adequately describe Easton, but it was the best her befuddled brain could come up with. And on top of that, he was chivalrous. Once again, she shot up a prayer of thanks and wondered what she'd done to deserve such good luck.

"This is such a beautiful town," she said, finally tearing her gaze away long enough to be charmed by the quaint buildings crowding the main street. "Do you know if the hotel — or sanitarium, or whatever it's called — is hiring? I can't stand the thought of just sitting around all day."

Easton graced her with a small smile, and Molly got the distinct impression he didn't bestow them easily. "Good to hear. And they are, but only maids and kitchen help. Is that okay?"

Molly grinned. "As the oldest of fifteen, I'm well-qualified for each of those positions."

He nodded his satisfaction and guided her up the steps to the church. Molly glanced back and saw the other couples following. Wait, not all of them. Sinead and her Mountie were nowhere to be seen. Miss Hazel scurried along ahead of the others to catch up with Molly and Easton.

"Wait for me!" the old woman cried.

Easton didn't hesitate. He swung open the door to usher Molly inside, where a minister stood at the altar in the process of marrying Sinead and Matthew. Molly jumped as organ music blared through the small church. A stout, pleasant-looking woman sat at an organ tucked in the corner of the room.

The second Sinead and Matthew left the altar, Easton practically dragged Molly down the aisle, barely giving her a moment to hug her friend as she passed. It seemed Matthew was in every bit of a hurry as Easton, because they were out the door before the others had caught up.

"Shouldn't we wait…" Molly started, looking back over her shoulder again. It didn't seem right to go through with this without her friends' support.

Easton remained mute, stopping only when he stood in front of the minister. "Pastor Franklin," he said with a nod. "Ready whenever you are."

"I appreciate your enthusiasm, Commander, but we need one more witness," the pastor said with a chuckle.

"That would be me!" Miss Hazel plowed through the door and hurried up the aisle as quickly as her stout legs could carry her. She stopped a few feet short of them, panting heavily. "If you would have…just…slowed down…a little…" she huffed, trying to catch her breath and fanning herself.

"Ready?" Pastor Franklin asked her. At her nod, he launched into his sermon.

For a moment, Molly wondered if she was bound for Hell for not having a traditional Catholic wedding, but then she caught Easton staring at her and her guilt melted away. God had seen fit to bring them together, and if anyone would know what kind of wedding options were available in Cougar Springs, it would be the Big Guy upstairs.

Molly smiled up at Easton, but instead of returning it, his eyes widened slightly and she could have sworn she heard a slight intake of breath. Then the pastor cleared his throat pointedly.

"Commander Cooper, I'll ask again, do you take this woman to be your lawfully wedded wife?"

Easton blinked, his eyes flicking back and forth between Pastor Franklin and Molly. "Oh. Um…yes. I do."

Molly's smile turned into a grin. She'd never had any kind of effect on a man before — at least, not to her knowledge — so to ruffle the most handsome man she'd ever laid eyes on *during* their wedding thrilled her beyond measure.

"Molly Hennessy, do you take this man to be your lawfully wedded husband?"

"You bet I do!"

Her friends snickered at her enthusiasm, but Easton looked at her as if he'd just discovered some crazy new species. Hopefully he would like her particular kind of crazy.

"You may kiss the bride."

Without hesitating, Molly closed her eyes and stood on her tippy toes, lips pursed and ready for her first real kiss. When it didn't come, she squinted one eye open to find Easton staring down at her again. Rather than wait for him to come to his senses, she reached up, wrapped her arms around his neck and pulled his head down to meet hers.

She'd only meant for it to be a quick smooch to seal the deal, but the second his lips touched hers, Molly's entire body turned to jelly. Whatever senses he had remaining were enough to hold her tight to his chest as their kiss deepened.

When he finally broke away, it was Molly who swayed on her feet, her fingers whispering along her burning lips. Tingles zipped along the nerves, bringing a hot flush to her face. She'd always wondered what all the fuss was about, and now that she knew, she wanted to do it again and again and again…

※

IT WAS Easton's duty as Commander of his team to witness all of their weddings — well, except overly-eager Matthew's — which gave him some much needed time to figure out what was going on inside him. Had he suddenly contracted the flu? Even though he'd only been a child at the time, he still remembered how quickly the Russian flu epidemic of 1890 had spread. Maybe Molly had infected him when they'd kissed.

That didn't make sense though. His stomach had started flip-flopping around like a fish on a riverbank the moment he'd laid eyes on her. Obviously Molly was the cause of his discomfort, but he simply didn't know why.

As Samuel and a pretty gal named Beth said their *I do's*, Easton dared to glance down at his new wife — the wife he hadn't really wanted in the first place. Tears slipped down her pink cheeks as she watched her friend seal her vows with a kiss, then she broke out in applause, grinning all the while.

What a strange creature. Crying and smiling at the same time? How was that even possible? Easton couldn't remember the last time he'd cried.

Darkness welled up in his belly, reminding him of the exact date he'd last shed tears. He pushed it back down into the depths and joined Molly in clapping. Then she beamed up at him, her grey eyes sparkling with joy, and the darkness fled.

"Would you like to see your new home?" he asked before his brain could stop him.

She nodded mutely, though Easton suspected that would not be a normal occurrence for Mrs. Molly Cooper. He'd never had a steady relationship with a woman before, but he'd had enough experience with the species to instinctively know this one was a talker. Sure enough, the minute they stepped outside the church, she started up.

"Never in my wildest dreams did I think I'd end up living in such a beautiful place," she said, sighing as she snaked her arm through his.

As she chattered away about how picturesque Cougar Springs was, he laid his hand atop the one clutching his red serge and marveled at its silky softness. The chill in it worried him though. They were having a bit of a warm spell, and most of the accumulated snow in town had melted away, but it was the middle of November and would turn quite cold very soon. If she was this cold now, she'd be freezing in a couple of weeks.

Wrapping his fingers around the tips of hers, he squeezed to bring some warmth to them. Only then did he notice the calluses hidden underneath, and wondered what had caused them. All he really knew about Molly was that she was skilled at housework and came from a large family.

"Oh my!" Molly exclaimed, stopping dead in her tracks. "That's the funniest looking deer I've ever seen!"

Easton followed her gaze and shook his head. "Reindeer."

"What?"

"That's a reindeer," he said, pointing to the animal he'd seen loitering about town. It stood placidly in a sunny spot, munching on some dead grass exposed by the melting snow. "Not a deer."

Almost as if the animal knew they were talking about him, he lifted his mighty rack of antlers and leveled his deep blue eyes on them as he chewed.

Molly gasped. "He's beautiful!"

Everything was beautiful to her, and suddenly Easton looked at the most mundane things differently, including the reindeer. His dusky hide blended into a creamy neck, which darkened into an almost regal face. His head was crowned by a massive set of antlers, and for the first time, Easton was impressed by the creature's majesty.

"Huh. Guess he is."

As placid as the dining reindeer appeared, it was still a wild animal. To be safe, Easton pulled Molly away toward his cabin, situated just past the Institute. "My cabin's modest, but it's clean and cozy. I like it that way, and I hope you do too."

Until she'd stepped off the train, he hadn't thought about whether she'd like his home, he'd only hoped she wouldn't change anything. He liked it just the way it was and he hoped she would too.

"I'm sure I will. I've never had a home of my own. I'm an excellent housekeeper, as I'm sure Miss Hazel must have mentioned. I learned from a frog, you know."

"A frog?"

"Yes. Whenever I went to wash the windows, he'd tell me to rub it, rub it, rub it."

Easton glanced down, puzzled for a moment, then it hit him that she'd just told a joke. And it was amusing. He smiled to show his appreciation.

"Here we are," he said as they stopped at the steps of his home. His heart had never pounded so hard in his life, waiting for her response. When she turned a smile on him, he felt as if he'd just won a gold medal at the Olympics.

"It's beautiful," she breathed, and for the first time, that's how it seemed to Easton.

A simple log cabin which had been built during the early days of the town, his home had been donated by the city to house the RNWMP commander. Remnants from the last snow had collected around the edges of the roof, giving it a gingerbread house appeal. The front porch had a roof to offer protection from the elements, as well as a comfortable spot to watch the town's goings-on when he was off duty.

"Shall we?" he asked.

"Heck yeah!" she said, starting for the steps, but he stopped her.

"Custom dictates I should carry you."

Her eyes grew wide. "Oh. Um, okay."

Easton bent low and picked her up in one easy movement. She barely weighed a thing, and he wondered how she'd hold up during the winter months. Then thoughts of her well-being vanished as he felt her tense against him.

"Are you okay?" he asked. "Would you rather—"

"No, I'm fine," she said, her teeth clamped tight.

When she wrapped her arms around his neck, he had to take a calming breath before daring to take the first step. Once he reached the door, he wondered who'd come up with this silly tradition. The man clearly hadn't thought about how the groom was supposed to open the door with two arms full of 'wife'.

Molly giggled as he struggled to turn the door knob, then gasped when he finally kicked it open. Turning her sideways, he swept through the doorway, imagining what a romantic figure they cut, when…

BONK!

"Ow!" Molly cried, slapping her hands to the spot on her head that had connected with the doorframe.

Easton rushed her to a chair and set her down carefully, then kneeled in front of her. "I'm so sorry! Are you hurt?"

"Well, that didn't feel like the kiss you gave me back in the church," she said, head down, as she rubbed her bruised scalp. When she finally met his gaze, her eyes twinkled. "But it really hit the spot."

"Hit the… Oh! Another joke. Cute."

Easton had never been one for jokes, mostly because he rarely understood them. As far as he was concerned, life was far too difficult to make fun of it. But he had to admit, Molly had a way of telling them that brought a smile to his lips — when he understood them.

"Are you sure you're okay? I could go fetch a doctor or nurse from the Institute."

"No, no," she said, waving a hand. "I'm fine. Really. I have some medical training."

This took Easton by surprise. Mounties were well-versed in first aid, but beyond treating minor injuries, the focus of his life had been upholding the law of the great land of Canada.

"See?" Molly said, holding out a hand. "It's not even bleeding. Barely a lump. My mother always said I had a hard head, and you just proved her right!"

Easton suspected as much, but was relieved nonetheless. When she tried to stand, he stopped her and took the seat across from her.

"Why don't we sit for a minute before I give you the grand tour, let you recuperate." She tried to object, but he held up a hand that cut off further discussion on the subject. "Tell me about your medical training."

At his request, Molly lit up like the Northern Lights, causing something to flutter in his stomach again.

"Oh! I'm a trained midwife."

"Really? You seem too young."

Molly straightened her back and tipped her nose up, as if he'd just insulted her, though he had no idea how she could have been offended by his comment. "I'll have you know I'm twenty-seven, Easton. I started my training when I was seventeen."

"Sev— Now *that* seems young."

She relaxed a little and sighed. "I suppose it was, but I didn't have much choice. It was the only way I could delay the inevitable."

Easton sat silently while his new bride chewed on her pretty pink lower lip. He'd learned long ago that staying silent often yielded far more answers than a constant barrage of questions.

"There's something else you should know about me," she finally said, her gaze not meeting his. "I was a nun."

Easton almost shoved his pinky in his ear and wiggled it around, thinking he'd misheard, but her grave expression told him he'd heard right.

"How…?" he sputtered, unable to find any words that would express the odd mix of emotions tumbling around inside him. "Why…? What…?"

Molly smiled and laid a cool hand on his, calming him instantly. "I really should have said I was *almost* a nun. I managed to talk my parents into letting me train as a midwife before joining the sisterhood. I convinced them it would help if I was sent on a mission of mercy. But I eventually had to start the process. All that was left was to say my final vows, but I married you instead."

He wasn't sure whether he should be honored or disgraced. The one thing he *was* sure about was that he had no idea how to treat her — not that he'd really known to begin with. No wonder she'd tensed in his arms — she'd probably never been held by a man before, much less kissed. That concerned him even more.

"I-I...uh... I see," he somehow managed to spit out. "Well, that being the case, perhaps we should wait to...perform our...um...*duties.*"

Easton's face burned like never before. He was always the level-headed one, the one who never got flustered. But he'd never married a nun before, either.

Molly's cheeks pinked up too, but she at least looked thoughtful. Her brow furrowed, then she looked him full in the eye. "No, I'm tired of waiting for my life to begin. But maybe we could wait until after I fix you a big dinner."

She jumped up and began exploring the small yet tidy kitchen, leaving Easton to stare after the whirlwind that was Molly Cooper. Easton didn't even mind that she was pulling all sorts of items from crates and cupboards and setting them willy-nilly on the counter. A beautiful woman was going to make him dinner, then make him her husband.

Hmm, maybe this marriage thing won't be so bad after all.

CHAPTER 3

Birds chirped all around Molly as she skipped down the steps of the Institute. It seemed more like a fancy hotel than a hospital, but maybe she'd try to find the medical section now that she'd been hired on as a maid. She was deeply curious about the magic healing waters she'd seen advertised.

"Stop that infernal racket," snapped an elderly man hobbling along the sidewalk as she passed.

Only then did Molly realize the birds she'd been hearing had actually been her own whistling. Surprised by the man's grouchiness, Molly apologized and hurried away from him, wondering why she should be sorry for being happy.

After an eternity of feeling as if her life was a dress that had been made for someone else, she almost felt comfortable in her own skin. Sure, a few of the fancy ladies in the hotel had given her the once-over, but that was nothing new.

What *was* new was the joy she felt in every breath she'd taken since stepping off the train the day before. A freedom she'd never experienced before almost overwhelmed her with gratitude for a chance at a life she'd always dreamed of.

Granted, she hadn't dreamed of becoming a maid, but helping to raise her fourteen younger brothers and sisters had taught her to be a fast and efficient housekeeper. And after cleaning Easton's already spotless cabin in just a few minutes, she realized she needed something more. A part-time job at the hotel would keep her busy while still allowing time for her duties at home, and Easton had seemed happy she wanted to work.

A mix of embarrassment and pleasure heated her face at the thought of 'duties'. Molly's mother had called it her "wifely duty" — much as Easton had — but it hadn't felt like a chore to Molly. Easton had been gentle and sweet with her, and she'd found herself enjoying her 'duties' more than she thought possible. Which, naturally, brought a fresh wave of guilt.

Molly had lived her entire life assuming she'd remain a virgin forever, and now that she wasn't...

She tried to shake off the guilt, but it clung to her like stink on a skunk. Not only was she married, she reminded herself, she'd been married by a man of God. Even though the ceremony wasn't Catholic, she felt sure God wasn't too worried about that. But no amount of logic could quell the conflicting emotions churning in her tummy.

Molly was so consumed with her own thoughts, she barely noticed the heavily pregnant woman who waddled by, going the opposite direction. As they passed, a creamy glove dropped to the ground, unnoticed by the woman.

Molly stooped and picked it up, astounded by the softness of the fabric against her rough fingers. Softer than butter. She'd never owned something so fine and doubted she ever would, but that didn't make her sad. She felt blessed to have had the chance to feel such suppleness at all.

Turning, she opened her mouth to call after the mother-to-be, when the woman spun around and snapped, "Give me that! It's mine!"

Without so much as a word of thanks, the woman snatched the glove from Molly's hand and stormed off as fast as her bulging body would allow.

Molly stared after her, aghast that the woman had thought Molly was a thief, and amused by the very same thing.

"What was that all about?" asked a voice behind her.

Sinead frowned after the woman, and Molly thought for a moment her friend might chase down the rude woman and make her apologize. Molly loved her for it, but she knew better than most that pregnant ladies became emotional very easily. She decided not to take offense, and snaked her arm through Sinead's, continuing in the direction she'd been walking before the strange encounter.

"Sinead, I need to apologize to you."

Sinead's dark eyes clouded over. "For what?"

"For being so unforgivably rude the first time we met."

"Oh, please don't—" Sinead started, but Molly cut her off.

"No, it was terrible of me, and I'm grateful that you've forgiven me. I also want to explain why I reacted the way I did."

Sinead said nothing for a few steps, then murmured, "Okay."

"You know I have fourteen siblings, right? We're your typical Irish Catholic family, and while I love them all fiercely, growing up in such a crazy household wasn't easy. On top of that, my father was a laborer, so we never had much more than what we needed to survive. We only went hungry a few times, that I can remember, but none of us really had anything that was ours and ours alone. Except for that shawl. It's the only thing I've ever owned outright, and it means more to me than…"

Emotions choked Molly's words, and Sinead wrapped a comforting arm around her shoulders, giving her the strength to continue.

"It's special to me, and when I saw you wearing it… Well, it reminded me of one of my sisters stealing my clothes, and I'm afraid I reacted poorly. I'm so sorry for that."

Sinead squeezed Molly's shoulder and smiled. "Don't give it a second thought, my friend. But I have to say, I'm honored that you thought of me as a sister, even if only for a split second."

A relieved laugh burst out of Molly. "It may have only been for a second *then*, but I feel that way all the time now."

They happily sauntered down the main street of town, arm in arm, and ignored the curious looks from passersby. They must have made quite the pair — Molly with her pale cream skin and flaming red hair, and Sinead with her dark skin and exotic features — but all Molly cared about was how happy she was.

"How lucky am I that I get to take two walks with you in one day?" Sinead asked, taking in the stunning landscape that lay around them, towering into the sky. "I never got the chance to ask you how married life is treating you."

Sinead grinned, as if the answer was written all over Molly's face.

It probably was.

"You were too busy insulting the Institute's doctor earlier," Molly said with a snort of laughter.

Sinead snorted too, but hers was disgusted, rather than amused. "*Doctor!* I'm convinced that man is a charlatan, and I'm going to prove it!"

Molly squeezed Sinead's arm. "Calm down, Dr. Sherlock. I believe you asked me a question, and the answer is…wonderfully."

Sinead stopped in her tracks and blinked at her friend. "Really? You were so nervous about…everything."

Molly didn't bother trying to hide her blush. Sinead knew her too well. "I know. But as with all things I worry about, it was for nothing."

Sinead bumped her with her hip and winked. "Told ya!"

"You were right," Molly said, rolling her eyes. "You're always right."

"Why can't you ever remember that?" Sinead raised her voice and looked around them. "I need a witness! Molly Cooper just admitted I'm *always* right!"

"I'll be your witness!" Miss Hazel rumbled up from behind, smiling broadly.

"Miss Hazel!" Molly and Sinead cried simultaneously as they hugged the older woman.

Miss Hazel positioned herself between them and linked arms so they took up almost the entire breadth of the sidewalk. "You girls look positively radiant!"

Molly and Sinead exchanged a conspiratorial glance and smiled as demurely as they could manage. Neither had thought it possible to fall so head over heels in just one day, but somehow they'd managed.

"And it's all thanks to you, Miss Hazel," Sinead said.

"Oh, pish posh! I'm just the middleman... middle*woman*. You do all the hard work of falling in love. Trust me, I was married for an eternity. I know exactly how hard marriage can be!"

"Well, you did well matching me with Easton," Molly said, her heart racing at the mere mention of her husband's name.

Miss Hazel's smile faltered for a fraction of a second. Or maybe Molly just imagined it. "I'm so glad. What about you Sinead?"

Sinead grimaced. "Well, I'm not sure if Matthew is satisfied with *me*, but I think he's the most wonderful man I've ever met."

Miss Hazel gasped and stopped to stare at Sinead. "Not satis— How could you say such a thing?! Rest assured, my dear, if Matthew doesn't quite see what a prize he's won, he soon will."

"Amen!" Molly added.

Sinead looked abashed and opened her mouth to speak, but her eyes popped open wide. "Oh! What's *that?*"

Molly and Miss Hazel followed the direction she pointed. A reindeer that looked suspiciously like the one she and Easton had seen the day before stood under a tree, munching on a mouthful of late-season grass.

"Oh, that's just Rocky," Miss Hazel said, as if that explained everything.

"Rocky?" Molly asked.

"Yes, Rocky. Don't you think he looks like a Rocky? I certainly do."

The Hennessy family had owned no fewer than three pets while Molly was growing up, all of them named after Catholic saints, but she'd never heard of naming a wild animal before. Still, it seemed like a lovely idea, especially if this particular reindeer had a habit of hanging around town.

"I don't know, Miss Hazel," Molly mused, cocking her head to one side to evaluate the creature. "He looks more like a Rudy to me."

"Rudy?!" Miss Hazel gasped. "What kind of name is that?"

"With that white goatee, he looks a little like my great-uncle Rudolph. You don't like it?"

Miss Hazel might as well have smelled a sack of rotten potatoes, judging by the face she made.

"Rocky it is!" Molly said, disentangling herself from the other two. "Now it's about time I go help Sinead start dinner, then get back to my house."

"What's the rush?" Sinead asked.

"I still need to unpack and see what I can do about making that sterile jail cell of a cabin into a home."

As she and Sinead turned away, Molly thought

she caught a glimpse of worry in Miss Hazel's eye. Or maybe Molly imagined that too.

※

"Now Ezekiel, I don't want to see you in here again for at least a week, got it?"

Easton entered the station just as Matthew unlocked the cell in the back, the large iron keyring clanging on the bars as he turned it. Poor ol' Ezekiel Chambers winced as the door screeched open and slapped his hands to his ears. He groaned in response. Easton sighed in pity as he settled himself behind his desk.

He'd served at several posts over his career as a Mountie, and there always seemed to be one resident in town who excelled at drinking. He didn't much care for the term 'town drunk', but others had been known to call them that. Zeke Chambers was theirs.

"Do my best, sir," Ezekiel mumbled as he brushed past Matthew. He staggered a little before catching himself on the edge of Easton's desk, where he paused to gather his bearings — or what was left of them.

"Rough night, eh Zeke?" Easton asked, leaning

back in his chair to distance himself from the foul odors wafting off their guest.

Ezekiel leveled a cold, unamused glare at him. "You could say that, cap'n."

"Commander. How many times do I have to tell you that, Zeke?"

Ezekiel shrugged and somehow managed to pull himself upright. No small feat, considering the state Nathaniel and Samuel reported the man to be in when they hauled him in to sleep it off. Again.

Matthew opened the door for Ezekiel, no doubt as a hint for him to finally leave, but also to air out the place. Easton felt Matthew's eyes on him and gave him a questioning glance.

"You sure seem to be in a good mood, boss," Matthew said, squinting at Easton with suspicion.

Easton shifted in his seat, but Ezekiel saved him with his smart mouth. "How can you tell that? He looks just as sour as ever."

Sour? Easton had no idea he looked sour. Professional, yes. Sour, no.

"Easy," Matthew explained, plopping into his chair and grinning. "He forgot to straighten his desk."

Ezekiel and Easton turned their gazes to the desk before them. Zeke probably didn't notice the inkwell in the wrong spot or the way his desk blotter sat slightly askew, but Easton did. *Now* he did. How had he missed it all? Matthew chuckled when Easton moved the inkwell to its proper place.

"Enough of that, now," Easton grumbled, shooting his constable a dark look.

Ezekiel yawned loudly and followed it up with a belch. "Well, better go see what Sam's serving up this morning."

Matthew called after him as the man stumbled out the door. "One week, Zeke! Y'hear?"

Ezekiel flapped a hand noncommittally as he disappeared.

"I need to say thanks," Matthew said after the stench followed Ezekiel out the door.

"For what?" Easton asked as he made sure everything on his desk was in the proper position.

"For agreeing to take a wife, even though you didn't really want one."

Easton couldn't have been more surprised if Matthew had punched him in the nose. His friend wasn't wrong, but he thought he'd hidden his uncertainty about the plan for them all to marry strange women quite well. Apparently not.

"You knew?"

Matthew smiled. "I work with you all day, every

day, Easton. I know you better than you think. Probably better than you know yourself."

Easton frowned at that, wondering how that could even be possible, but then the warmth of friendship enveloped him. It wasn't an entirely comfortable sensation for Easton. He'd jumped around from post to post, barely staying at any of them long enough to remember his co-workers' names, much less develop deep friendships with any of them. He'd been at Cougar Springs longer than usual, though, and he'd grown closer to his men than he'd ever thought possible.

"Oh yeah?" he shot back at Matthew. "What am I thinking right now?"

Matthew squinted, as if he was concentrating hard, then his eyes snapped open and he gasped in mock shock. "Why, Easton Cooper! How dare you think such rude things!"

Matthew's laughter filled the room and, as usual, left Easton feeling like he had found a home. Even his commanding officer back in Regina had noticed, and not-so-subtly implied Cougar Springs could be Easton's permanent posting, if he wanted. He hadn't given it much thought before, but he suddenly realized he must have wanted that all along or he wouldn't have sent away for a bride.

"So, is your wife everything you thought she'd be?" he asked Matthew.

"And then some," Matthew said with a half-laugh, half-sigh. "Did you know she's a doctor?"

"And that's a problem because…" Easton had been thrilled to learn Molly was a midwife, and he liked the idea of a *real* doctor residing in Cougar Springs. He didn't trust that slimy Dr. Jenkins, the so-called doctor who ran the Institute.

"It's not a problem, I just…wasn't expecting it. As you can imagine, she has a mind of her own, and I swear she's going to be the death of me. Or herself."

Easton winked. "Match made in heaven, you ask me."

Matthew scowled at him from across the room, then lifted an eyebrow. "And what about you? Has your lovely new bride made a mess of your life yet?"

Easton gave him a smug smirk. "Impossible. She only brought one small case, barely big enough to hold a dress. No, sorry to disappoint you."

Matthew snorted. "We'll see about that. She's barely been here a day."

"She won't have time, if she gets that job she was talking about."

"Job? As a midwife? Is there room enough for two midwives in Cougar Springs, or is she planning to put old Stella out of job?"

Easton shook his head. "No, as a maid. She took one look around my place and immediately wondered what she'd do all day. When she brought up working at the hotel, I was all for it."

"Really? You *want* her working for Jenkins?"

Guilt chewed at him for allowing his wife to work for such a viper. "No, but she won't be working directly under him," Easton reasoned. "I'm sure the manager, Mr. Jackson, will be her immediate superior." What he didn't add was that he rather liked the idea of them living more independently from each other than was expected of a married couple. Maybe marriage wouldn't be so disruptive to his carefully ordered life after all.

Matthew opened his mouth to say something when a woman stomped through the open door. A very pregnant woman who was breathing hard and looked redder than a beet. Easton jumped to his feet and rushed to her side.

"May I help you to a chair, ma'am?"

The woman huffed her agreement and took a moment to collect herself before launching into her reason for coming. Easton wondered if she might be in labor, judging by her heavy breathing, but she calmed herself after a few moments and the cup of water Matthew offered her.

"Thank you," she said, laying a pair of white gloves in her lap. "I came to file a report against a thief."

Easton nodded at Matthew to take notes while he questioned the woman. Silent communication was just one more benefit of becoming close to one's co-workers.

"What did you have stolen, Mrs...?"

"Mrs. Constance Hildebrand," she answered tartly. "And *this* is what was stolen."

She flapped a solitary glove in Easton's face. He took it because that seemed to be what she wanted, and he marveled at its softness. Cashmere, if he wasn't mistaken. Handing it back, he moved his chair around in front of her.

"Tell me what happened, Mrs. Hildebrand."

"I was out for my daily walk, as Dr. Jenkins prescribed— You know Dr. Jenkins, don't you?" She flicked her head back with a sniff. "He's my personal physician."

Easton avoided glancing at Matthew, not that he needed to. Neither considered Jenkins much of a doctor.

"Go on," he urged.

"I was out for my walk, my gloves firmly clasped in my hands, when I suddenly realized one was missing. They were a gift from my husband, you see, so I'm very careful about keeping track of them."

"Mmm hmm."

"I turned around to look for it, thinking I must have dropped it, when I saw this ragamuffin of a girl fondling *my* glove!"

Easton's eyebrows pulled together in confusion. "So you dropped your glove, and a child picked it up?"

The woman huffed so loudly it was almost a shout. "No! She wasn't a child! She was a full grown woman, and a thief to boot. She must have snatched the glove from me as we passed. I *knew* there was no way I could have dropped it!"

"So…this woman, she was trying to get your other glove and that's how you noticed what had happened?"

This time Mrs. Constance Hildebrand threw her hands in the air. "No! Are you not listening to me? She was just standing there, *fondling* my glove!"

Easton could no longer resist casting a dubious glance at Matthew, who looked just as confused as Easton felt.

"How did you get the glove back, if I might ask?"

"I took it from her, of course!"

Easton rubbed his brow, trying to make sense of her story. "So what you're telling me is that while you were walking down the sidewalk, you noticed one of your gloves was gone, then you turned around and saw a woman standing behind you with the glove in her hand?"

Mrs. Hildebrand gave him a curt nod. "That's right. She stole it and I took it back, and I want to press charges, Commander!"

"But you got the glove back," Matthew interjected. At the mother-to-be's withering glance, he clammed up.

"Can you tell me what this woman looked like?"

"Yes, she was smallish, with bright red hair and colorless eyes. She wore a reddish shawl around her shoulders. A thief if I ever saw one."

Color rose in Easton's face. "I believe you're talking about my wife, Mrs. Hildebrand," he said so quietly he barely heard himself speak

Her previously defiant eyes flashed with alarm. "Oh! Well, I…" Faster than he thought possible, she launched her bulk from the chair and hurried to the door. "I didn't mean to insult your wife, Commander, but you really should keep better control of her."

Before the hem of her dress swept out of sight, Easton was on his feet, heading for home. He needed to get to the bottom of this, and only Molly could tell him what really happened. He didn't believe for a minute she stole the woman's glove, but it wouldn't do for rumors to start that the commander's wife was a thief.

Throwing the door of their cabin open, Easton stopped cold and looked around his home in disbelief. His table and chairs, which he'd carefully located directly opposite the fireplace against the wall, now stood in the middle of the room and at a cockeyed angle. A tin cup brimming with scruffy pale flowers — no doubt riddled with insects and dirt — sat atop the table, just off center and nestled far too close to a lit candle.

Tiny knickknacks he'd never seen before littered almost every flat surface in the cabin, and he couldn't help wondering how she'd managed to fit all that junk into one small bag. Draped over two unevenly pounded nails hung Molly's prized shawl. The woman herself grinned over her shoulder at him as she hung a freshly cut bough of pine over the mantel.

A twitch started in Easton's right eye, then moved down to his cheek. His home...she'd ruined it! He tried to find words to express himself, but they eluded him. He finally spit out the only words that came to mind.

"Enough of that, now!"

CHAPTER 4

Molly had spent the better part of the afternoon doing what she could to spruce up the stark cabin. Aside from moving the table and chairs closer to the fire so she wouldn't freeze to death during meals, she wasn't able to do much with what she had. Some late-blooming purple asters, which had somehow managed to escape Rocky the Reindeer's foraging, brightened up the room a touch, but the chipped and rusted tin can she found to hold them was only slightly better than nothing.

She'd practiced poverty as a novice in the convent — which hadn't taken much practice since she'd grown up poorer than dirt — so she owned very little in the way of personal effects. Her shawl, of course, but each of her brothers and sisters had given her a small, handmade going-away present on the eve of her departure. Most people in Cougar Springs would look at the trinkets and see garbage, but they were priceless to Molly. She was proud to decorate her new home with them.

A hearty stew simmered on the stove for dinner, and Molly thought the candle on the table would be a nice touch for when Easton came home, but the walls needed...*something.* With no paintings or family photographs to hang, Molly had again worked with what she had: her beautiful scarf and a cutting from a fragrant pine tree just outside their door. It wasn't much, but she'd transformed the sparse cabin into a cozy home that made her heart swell with joy and satisfaction.

Then Easton came home.

Molly's happy grin faltered when she saw red flooding into Easton's face as he stood in the doorway, glowering. His eyes grew round as he scanned the room, then his mouth started popping open and closed like a fish on a riverbank. When he finally spoke, it wasn't words of praise for her handiwork — as she'd expected — and his tone sounded less than pleased.

"What?" She couldn't have heard him right. He had to have said something other than—

"Enough of that, now," he growled, his voice growing louder. He stepped inside and slammed the door behind him.

Molly jumped at the noise, utterly confused. He actually seemed angry…with *her!* "What's wrong?"

Easton's lips pressed into a hard line. "I didn't give you permission to change anything in my home."

Molly flicked her gaze around at the minor changes she'd made. Her confusion was replaced with a more familiar, and infinitely more unsavory, emotion. "Excuse me? What did you just say to me?"

The spark caught in her chest, and the flames of anger skittered up her neck like wildfire. As soon as it reached her mouth, Molly knew from experience, all bets would be off. She'd hoped to hide her volatile temper from her groom for a little while longer, but this attack hit her doubly hard since it was so unexpected *and* unwarranted.

"Didn't you understand my instructions?" Easton demanded, jamming his fists onto his hips. Standing there in his Mountie uniform, he once again looked as if he stepped out of a recruitment poster — only his attitude was less than impeccable.

Molly clenched her teeth and balled up her fists

to ward off her bad side. "What instructions?" she asked through pursed lips.

"Yesterday, on our way here. I told you I liked my place just the way it was, and to not do anything to change that."

The fire finally reached Molly's eyes, turning the world red, and her full fury poured forth. "You mean on our way here after our *wedding?* What *I* remember is you saying that you liked to keep *our* house clean, and you could eat off these floors, Mr. Mountie Man!"

Easton blinked at the words she spat at him, and a small, quiet part of her wished she could stop, but now that she was consumed by the inferno...

"Are you really that upset I moved the table?" she demanded, advancing on him. It probably looked quite comical, a tiny woman glaring up at a very large man, but it didn't seem the least bit funny to Molly.

"I-I...liked it where it was," he muttered lamely.

"Well, *I* like it here!" She felt her nostrils flaring like a winded horse, but stood her ground.

"What about all this other nonsense?" He waved a hand around the room as he clearly tried to hold on to his indignation for as long as possible. The poor man had no idea who he was up against.

"Nonsense? *Nonsense!*"

Molly stomped over to the mantel and picked up a small snowman painstakingly sculpted from flour paste. Even in her anger, she handled the delicate trinket carefully.

"This *nonsense* was made for me by my sister, Sarah. She's seven." She set down the snowman and picked up a pinecone with a merry hat and twigs glued on for arms. "And this bit of *nonsense* is the genius of my little brother, Aiden. That *nonsense* is from another of my brothers, and that little thing is from another sister. I'd hoped one day you'd get to meet them all, but if this is how you think of the gifts they gave to me the last time I saw them, maybe I don't want you meeting them after all."

Easton stood stock still, mouth hanging open. Molly glared at him until he looked away and found his voice. "I just like things a certain way, is all," he mumbled to the floor.

"Has it ever occurred to you that I do too? This is my home as well, Easton Cooper, and I want it to *feel* like home, not a Siberian prison cell! If you don't like that, maybe you should just leave!"

The tension between them dragged out for about a decade, then Easton spun on his black boot heel and slammed out of the door without a word, or even a look back.

Molly stared at the door for a moment, the fire burning inside extinguished by the puff of cool air Easton's sudden departure let in. Dropping into one of the contested chairs, she stared into the fireplace and wondered what she'd just done. She had promised Mother Superior to take a deep breath and pray before losing her temper, but that was hard to remember when she could barely think straight.

All sense of time evaporated, so Molly had no idea how long she'd sat there before a knock sounded on the door. Leaping for the door, she wrenched it open.

"Easton, I—"

Miss Hazel stood before her. Her smile fell away, replaced by a worried frown. "Is everything okay, Molly?"

Molly glanced behind Miss Hazel, hoping to see Easton skulking about, but she only saw Rocky swaying down the street in the distance.

"No...I mean, yes. Fine. Come in."

Molly offered her guest some tea, but Miss Hazel gently pushed her into the chair she'd just vacated, then lowered herself into the chair across the table from her.

"Tell me what's wrong, and don't try to deny it. You've always worn your heart on your sleeve, Molly."

Just as suddenly as the fire had consumed Molly, guilt and sorrow poured from her eyes in a flood of tears. "I was so horrible to Easton, Miss Hazel! He was surprised, was all, but I flayed him open like a butcher. I wouldn't be surprised if he sent me back with you when you leave."

The older woman heaved her bulk out of the chair and pulled Molly's head to her bosom, stroking her hair and hushing her softly. "Shh… there there. We'll work it out. You can trust that, my dear."

With tremendous effort, Molly wrangled control of her emotions and pulled away. Once Miss Hazel had settled back in her seat, Molly explained everything, including how she'd told her new husband to get out of his own house.

"It's hopeless, isn't it, Miss Hazel? I've lost him forever, and it's all my fault!"

Fresh tears threatened, but Miss Hazel's light chuckle stopped them.

"Oh, Molly, my dear. Don't be so dramatic. It

was an argument, that's all. The first of many, I'd wager, knowing you as I do."

Molly's face heated up from shame at her renowned temper. But hope bloomed deep inside.

"You think so?"

"Of course, I do! Do you think Mr. Hughes and I never argued? We were as blissfully happy as any couple we knew, all the way to the end, but we were two separate people with separate needs and desires. Most of the time, they meshed well, but not always. Marriage isn't easy, Molly. It requires a goodly amount of give and take."

"And here I was taking, taking, taking." Molly dropped her head and picked at a flaking cuticle, unable to meet Miss Hazel's gaze.

"Poppycock! Molly Cooper, you're one of the least selfish people I've ever known. Other than letting your emotions get the better of you, you did nothing wrong. You have every right — no, you have a *responsibility* to make this a warm, cozy home for the both of you. As well as any little ones that might come along."

Molly's eyes snapped open at the mention of children, one of her heart's deepest desires. But first things first. "So…I wasn't being selfish by decorating?"

Miss Hazel smiled and patted her hand. "Not at all. Easton is lucky to have you, and he'll come to see that in time. You just need to let him get used to the idea of sharing his life with someone else. He seems to be the type of man who's taken care of himself for most of his life. He's not used to someone else filling that role."

"I never thought of it like that before," Molly mused, recalling Easton's brief mention of not having any family deep in the dark of night as she lay in his arms. If her suspicions were correct, Miss Hazel was spot on about him. "I swear I'll do better at controlling my temper, Miss Hazel. Thank you."

Miss Hazel waved away her words and looked around the cabin. "Now, you said something about tea? I don't suppose you have any cookies to go with it…"

"COMMANDER, WHAT A PLEASANT SURPRISE!"

Sam Bonney welcomed Easton into her saloon and escorted him to his usual table. ChiChi sat on her shoulder, grinning and chattering at Easton. The monkey was amusing, but Easton was happy Sam kept the animal under control.

"I thought for sure you'd be holed up for the next month or so with your new bride."

She tipped him a wink. Ignoring the insinuation, he placed his hat on the table and sat with a grunt.

"Beer, please."

Sam gasped, causing ChiChi to screech and leap to a wall sconce. Ignoring the monkey, she sat across from him, eyeing him hard. "Is everything okay, Commander? You never drink anything harder than iced tea."

Easton sighed and rubbed his forehead, and before he knew what was happening, he was spilling his guts to the saloon owner. Since the dawn of time, men shared their woes with bartenders, so he shouldn't be any different — but he'd always thought he was.

"This marriage was a terrible idea. I knew better, but my men all wanted wives and they wouldn't have done it on their own if I hadn't agreed. Who marries a woman he's never met?"

Sam opened her mouth to reply, but he didn't give her time.

"Better question: who marries a man *she's* never met? A wild Irish lass who refuses to obey my very clear instructions, that's who."

"Tell me what happened," Sam said quietly, ignoring the bustle of the bar around them.

Easton chewed on the inside of his cheek for a moment, wondering if sharing such personal information with another woman was proper. Unfortunately, he had no one else to share it with. He couldn't show such weakness in front of his men. Besides, he'd always listened whenever Sam needed to complain about her own husband.

"I told her I liked things just so, but I came home — to find out why someone had accused her of *stealing*, no less — and she'd changed everything! It didn't even look like my own home anymore. She only brought one small case the nuns at the convent gave her, yet there were knickknacks everywhere. How did she fit it all in there? Plus, she moved the furniture and…"

"And?" Sam pressed when he hesitated.

Easton sighed with exasperation. "And when I made my displeasure known, she yelled at me. Now what kind of way is that for a bride to treat her new husband?"

Sam leaned back, arms crossed, as she regarded him. He shifted in his seat under her gaze as the seconds ticked by. Finally, she leaned forward, bracing her forearms on the table.

"I've known you a long time, Commander," she said, a smile playing at her lips, "and I don't believe I've ever seen you this unnerved. I've watched men train their guns on you, right in this very room, and you barely batted an eye. But that little wisp of a thing you married has you tied in knots."

"Exactly!" Thank goodness someone saw his point of view!

"More power to her, I say," Sam said, scooching her chair back and starting to rise.

"What? Why!" A few men glanced over at the pair, but Easton ignored them. He needed to find out what Sam meant by that.

She must have seen his distress and settled back in the chair. "Commander, you're used to being in control, having everyone obey you, no questions asked."

"That's right. I'm the commander of this Mountie force, and I can't have anyone challenging me. Chaos would descend otherwise."

Sam smiled softly and clicked her tongue. ChiChi landed on her shoulder and accepted a pet from her mistress.

"The one thing you forgot, Commander, is that this young woman is your *wife*, not your subordinate or a criminal. She's not under your command.

Unless she's breaking the law, she's free to live her life as she sees fit, and she's chosen to live it with you."

Easton frowned, wondering if Sam would ever get to her point. "And?"

"And...you can't expect her to obey your every whim."

"But she vowed to obey me," he objected, and even to his own ears, he sounded like a whining child.

"As you vowed to obey *her*, if I'm not mistaken."

Easton focused on ChiChi instead of meeting Sam's eyes. He let his silence answer for him. She sighed in disappointment, and for some reason, Easton felt as if his mother had just chided him. Which was ridiculous because he'd never had a mother.

"Okay, Commander, why don't you look at it from her point of view? What's her name again?"

"Molly," he muttered petulantly, though just saying her name made his lips tingle.

"Molly gave up everything she's ever known and everyone she's ever loved to live with a man she'd never met. Think about that for a moment. Can you imagine how absolutely terrifying that must have been for her?"

Easton couldn't help picturing Molly quaking with anxiety over what her new husband would be like. Would he be kind? Would he be violent? Was he who he said he was? Would she be accepted in town? With all his traveling as a Mountie, he could certainly relate to that last one. Every time he received orders to move to a different post, anxiety gnawed at his guts, and he wondered if he would be able to effectively lead his new team.

"Hmm…" he mused.

"If you ask me, she's incredibly brave. Maybe even braver than a Mountie."

Guilt stabbed his heart at her jibe, but he deserved it.

"And now you're telling me she was in a convent before this? Commander, Molly's world has been flipped upside down and inside out. And that small case of hers? You can bet your life it contained everything she owns. Every single thing. All she wanted to do was display her things so she wouldn't feel so isolated. She just wanted to make *your* home her home too. And you yelled at her for it?"

Easton had never been overly emotional, but something was trying to choke him from the inside. He prayed Sam would stop, but she kept right on. He could only be grateful that she kept her voice low so as to not make a scene. This justified humiliation was punishment enough.

"Commander, I know you like to control every aspect of your life, but if you want this marriage to work, you're going to have to become a willow tree and bend until you both find your footing." She gave him a steely look. "Do you want this marriage to work?"

Two days before, Easton would have quickly and easily answered 'No'. But from the moment he'd laid eyes on the fiery redhead who he'd instantly known would be his bride, everything had changed. A part of him he'd thought had died long ago had sparked to life again. Food tasted better, the sky was a little bluer, birds chirped a little louder. Imagining what his life would be like without Molly there to mess things up opened a hole in his heart he knew he'd never be able to fill again.

"I do, Sam. I honestly do."

Sam grinned and slapped the table, drawing a scolding from ChiChi. "Good! Now get on home and tell her that!"

Easton was out the door before she'd finished. As he hurried back to their cabin, he wondered for the first time if Molly would *want* to stay. After the way he treated her, he wouldn't blame her if she'd packed up that small case and was ready to leave on the next train.

Warm light shone through the windows as he climbed the steps, giving him hope she was still there, but he wasn't looking forward to the tongue lashing he knew he deserved. Hopefully, she would accept his apology eventually.

Bracing himself for the worst, he eased the door open and peeked inside, ready to duck a frying pan if need be. Instead, he was greeted by a smiling Molly standing next to a table loaded with the most delicious meal he'd ever smelled.

"Welcome home," she said meekly.

"What's all this?"

"I wanted to make my husband dinner."

Easton spent the moment it took to hang his hat wondering what exactly had happened in his absence. "I thought you'd still be angry with me."

"Well, I—"

"Never mind that," he said, moving to her and taking her hands in his. "I'm sorry, Molly. I was selfish and unforgivably rude to you. I have no real excuse, except that I grew up in an orphanage and had to fend for myself all my life. I'm not telling you this to make you feel sorry for me, just to shed some light on why I am…the way I am. You have every right to make this your home too. If you still want to, that is."

Her eyes misted over and she pulled her hands free to wrap them around his neck and pull him into the sweetest kiss he'd ever had in his life. When they broke apart, she gazed up at him with a light in her eyes that made his heart swell.

"I'm sorry too, Easton. I have a terrible temper and I swear I'll work hard to keep it in check."

He smiled down at his beautiful wife and wondered what he'd done in his life to deserve such an amazing woman.

"Does that mean you'll stay and turn this into *our* home?"

Molly grinned, then grabbed one of his hands and pulled him toward the bedroom. "Maybe later."

CHAPTER 5

"I'd love to quit, but I need something to do or I'll go crazy," Molly told Sinead as they walked past the crowded hot springs. Institute guests frolicked in the steaming waters as if it was a lovely summer day, instead of a dim late fall afternoon with clouds threatening more snow.

"It still reminds you of cleaning up after your dozens of siblings?" Sinead snickered, but not in a cruel way.

"The last three weeks have felt like my entire youth all over again, only with slightly less fighting. You would be shocked at how rich people treat others, much less their hotel rooms. Why, just the other day, I was changing the bedclothes when I found this huge—"

Sinead stuck her fingers in her ears and shouted, "La la la la! I don't want to know!"

They clung to each other for support as they laughed and walked, marveling in the white majesty surrounding them. Not long after the brides had arrived in Cougar Springs, the first snows had fallen, and they'd fallen ever since. No blizzards yet, but that was only a matter of time.

"How are things working out with the new head of the Institute?" Molly asked.

"Quite well. Ever since Dr. Porter replaced that quack Jenkins, I have more patients than time. And people are actually getting better."

"That's wonderful!"

"I can't believe what passed for medical care before we got here."

Molly snorted. "I think Rocky the Reindeer offered better medical care than Dr. Jenkins. You wouldn't believe how rude he was to the staff. Everyone hated him."

Sinead rolled her eyes. "Doesn't surprise me a bit, although I have to admit I'm surprised that *you* hated him. I know you have a temper, but I didn't think the word 'hate' was in your vocabulary."

"I never said *I* hated him, but I certainly didn't

like him very much. May the good Lord forgive my dark thoughts."

Sinead bumped her with her hip. "Molly, I doubt your thinking poorly of a bad man has even made God's list of sins."

"Maybe," Molly said, hoping it was true. "Tell me more about your practice."

Sinead shrugged. "At first, most of my patients were locals who'd developed a healthy aversion to the not-so-good doctor. It's taken a while, but the Institute patients seem to trust me now too."

"Any more babies being born? I'd surely love to take part, if I could."

"Stella takes care of them, mostly. She's only called me in once since that first time. But I worry about her. I get the sense she's tired, and at her age, I don't blame her. But I swear I'll send Matthew to fetch you the next time one comes up. As kind-hearted as Stella is, I'd feel better with you there."

"Aww," Molly said, flushing with pride that her friend trusted her more than the local midwife who'd been practicing for decades.

"So, how are things at home these days? I don't suppose Easton has suddenly become a slob."

"You know better than that," Molly said with a chuckle. "We're both working hard to learn how to live with each other. No one ever tells you about that part, do they? You grow up thinking your real life begins when you get married, but really it's just the same life, only now you have to tiptoe around to protect someone else's feelings."

"Are you two still arguing?"

"Not too much, but occasionally he'll try to order me around like I'm one of his men, and when I snap back, he runs off to the saloon."

Sinead gasped in surprise, and Molly quickly corrected her assumption.

"He only eats there, never drinks. I've met the proprietress, Sam, and she's a strong woman who doesn't mince words. She also runs a relatively respectable place. Well, as respectable as a saloon can be, I suppose."

A woman ahead of them caught Molly's eye. She looked familiar, and as they drew nearer, Molly recognized her as the heavily pregnant woman who'd accused Molly of stealing the glove she'd dropped, Mrs. Hildebrand. She was speaking to a tall, thin man Molly had never seen before.

His slicked-back dark hair and perfectly styled handlebar mustache almost reminded Molly of a melodrama villain. He stood behind a flimsy table loaded with all sorts of bottles, showing each to the woman in turn. Molly couldn't stop herself from listening in as she and Sinead passed.

"And this one will ease the ache in your lower back," the man said, his voice smooth and oozing with guile. "The three medicines— Don't be shy, ladies. Join us."

Molly started when she realized he was talking to her and Sinead. She shot her friend a glance and knew immediately Sinead was as curious about this man as she was. He was no doubt yet another quack trying to take advantage of those coming to the hot springs looking for a cure to whatever ailed them.

"My name is Dr. Joseph Kinderhawk, inventor of Dr. Kinderhawk's Miraculous Medicines. As you can see, this lovely young lady before me is expecting a miracle of her own any day now. Mrs. Hildebrand wisely came to me seeking relief from the many discomforts of her condition, and I'm happy to say I can help. I can help you too."

"Just tell me how much for all three," Mrs. Hildebrand demanded, obviously irritated the women had interrupted her transaction.

"Of course," Kinderhawk said, smiling and turning his full attention the rude woman. "So, a bottle Magnificent Mother's Milk to prepare yourself for the delivery, along with the Ultimate Unguent for your backaches and the Soothing Syrup to help you sleep. And because you're so near to welcoming your new bundle of joy, I will throw in, at absolutely no charge, a sample of my special Baby's Lullaby Elixir, to calm colicky infants."

The price he quoted the woman nearly made Molly faint, but the fact he was trying to con the poor lady riled her up even more than his outrageous prices. As Mrs. Hildebrand reached into her coat pocket to pay, Sinead snatched up one of the bottles while Molly laid a hand on the woman's arm.

"Ma'am, don't listen to him. He's a charlatan, a fraud. Whatever he's selling you won't help your condition, and it may harm you."

"Now listen here—" Kinderhawk objected, just as Sinead pulled the stopper from the bottle labeled *Magnificent Mother's Milk* and took a deep sniff.

"Phew!" she said, squinching her face up in distaste. "Grain alcohol, with maybe a hint of mint and camphor thrown in for good measure."

"The ingredients in my patented medicines are proprietary," Kinderhawk insisted, his desperate eyes darting from Sinead to Molly, then over to Mrs. Hildebrand. "They're proven effective!"

"Says you," Molly snorted.

"Take your hands off me!" Mrs. Hildebrand said, wrenching her arm away. "You're that little thief who tried to steal my glove. Go on, shoo! Leave me to my business and mind your own."

Kinderhawk smiled at Mrs. Hildebrand, while shooting a triumphant glare at Sinead and Molly. "Let me package these up for you while to find your coin purse, my good lady. Please ignore these dubious doubters."

"Ma'am," Sinead said, "these medicines could hurt you and your baby."

The woman huffed, and looked Sinead up and down, much as she had Molly weeks before. "How would *you* know?"

"Because I'm a doctor. A *real* doctor, not some imposter who tacked on the title to his own name. If that's even his real name. I can tell you that this one—" she picked up the unguent "—is made up of nothing more than petroleum jelly and camphor, and the one meant for your newborn baby almost certainly contains opium. Isn't that right *Mister* Kinderhawk?"

Kinderhawk grew red-faced and blustery. "I told you, the ingredients—"

"Yeah, yeah," Molly interrupted. "You just

don't want people to know how useless or dangerous they are."

"That's a lie!" He stormed around the table to confront her.

Molly stood her ground and glared up at him with the full might of her fury. "You're the liar! Your fake medicines could hurt this woman *and* her child! You're a fraud who should be run out of town on a rail!"

Kinderhawk loomed over her, his fists at the ready. "And who's gonna make me?"

Molly's vision turned red, and before she knew what was happening, she leapt at the man, fists pounding and fingernails scratching. The attack only lasted a few seconds before strong arms enveloped her and pulled her off Kinderhawk.

"Enough of that, now," a familiar voice growled in her ear, and Molly calmed in an instant. Easton was here. He'd take care of everything.

"Mountie, I want that woman arrested," screeched a hysterical Kinderhawk. "Just look what she did to me!"

The formerly tidy 'doctor' was no longer so tidy. His slick hair wasn't just mussed, it was actually...*crooked*! Before she could stop herself, Molly barked out a loud laugh.

"Is that a *wig?*"

Kinderhawk quickly adjusted the hairpiece, but it still sat slightly askew. "It's called a toupee, you halfwit!"

Easton stepped forward and bumped the man with his chest. "Easy now, that's my wife. Now what's going on here?"

Everyone but Mrs. Hildebrand spoke at once, and somehow Easton managed to listen to all of them. Finally, he turned to Kinderhawk with an expression that would have sent a bear running.

"Out," he said quietly.

"Excuse me?"

"Don't make me repeat myself again. Get out. Out of town this very day, or you'll regret every minute you stay here in Cougar Springs — because it will be in a cell. I've seen dozens of your kind pass through here, and I've seen even more trusting people duped into buying your junk. I'll say it one more time so you hear it right…"

Easton stepped so close to Kinderhawk the man had to tip his head back to look up into Easton's glowering face. "Out."

It was barely a whisper, but Kinderhawk jumped as if Easton had shouted. Within seconds, he'd packed up his bottles and was practically sprinting for the train station. They all watched his retreating form until he disappeared from view.

"So…" Mrs. Hildebrand ventured quietly, "he really was a fake?"

"I'm afraid so, ma'am," Easton said. "I'm sorry about all of this. But Mrs. Montgomery is a doctor, and my wife is a midwife. They were only trying to help you."

Mrs. Hildebrand turned to the women, her eyes misting up. "I'm sorry for not believing you, ladies. I'm just so tired and uncomfortable, and the hot springs aren't helping at all."

Easton shifted his feet as the woman broke down in tears. Molly patted his arm, then pulled Mrs. Hildebrand into a deep, comforting hug. "Don't think of it again, dear one. Shh…"

After a few minutes of uncontrolled sobbing, Mrs. Hildebrand finally composed herself. Easton proffered a handkerchief, which set Molly's heart pounding. Always the gentleman!

"I need help," Mrs. Hildebrand murmured, then caught Molly's gaze. "I don't suppose you would be willing to come stay with me until the baby's born, or until my husband returns in a week's time? I have a full suite in the Institute, and I'll pay you handsomely."

The fee she quoted sent Molly reeling backward until she bumped into her husband. His warmth seeped into her, giving her the strength she needed. "That's more than I earn in a month cleaning rooms, and you can't be more than a week away from giving birth!"

"Your lips to the good Lord's ears. Is it a deal?"

Molly could barely believe her good fortune. More than anything, she wanted to use her skills as a midwife, but she had a husband to think about now. She turned hopeful eyes up to him. "Is it all right with you?"

He brushed a lock of her tousled hair from her forehead. "I know how important this is to you. I'll miss you."

She stood on her tiptoes and kissed him full on the mouth, ignoring Mrs. Hildebrand's shocked gasp and Sinead's snicker. Warm tendrils snaked around her heart as he responded, pulling her close to him. When they finally broke apart, she whispered into his ear.

"Now you can arrange the house any way you like. Just be careful of my things when you put them away."

Surprise flashed across his face for a moment, then he grinned. "I promise."

After escorting Molly to Mrs. Hildebrand's suite of rooms, Easton's first stop was the station, where he instructed Matthew to make sure the fake doctor boarded the next train out. His second stop was Sam's.

"Here ya go, Commander," Sam said, setting a plate in front of him. "And your iced tea, as usual."

The steak still sizzled and the steaming baked potato melted a huge hunk of butter. Perfection! The tantalizing combined scents caused his stomach to rumble in anticipation of the tasty meal. Not that Molly wasn't a wonderful cook, but this dinner seemed special to Easton. He'd taken a few meals at Sam's since Molly blew into his life like a tornado, but he'd barely tasted the food because he'd been brooding over whatever argument they'd just had. The meal before him was a reminder of a time before, a time that seemed so far away, yet just out of reach.

Reaching for his glass, he stopped and smiled. A huge icicle stuck out of it, acting as the 'ice' in his iced tea.

"Cute," he said to Sam, who was in the process of settling herself in the chair across from him.

She shrugged. "I work with what I got. We don't get much call for iced tea this time of year, Commander, but you know I always keep a pitcher of it made up just for you."

"Thanks, Sam." Easton cut his first hunk of steak and popped it into his mouth with a smile. The smile faltered as he chewed the leathery steak. Strange…usually Sam's food was impeccable.

"You seem to be in a better mood than the last few times you've been in," Sam said, leaning back to appraise him.

"Molly was hired by a mother-to-be to stay with her for a week or so. Said I could put the cabin back to rights while she's gone."

"Ah, and you can't wait for your life to return to normal, is that right?"

Easton pointed his fork at Sam and winked as he chewed…and chewed and chewed. He gulped down half the glass of tea just to wash it down. To cleanse his palate, he dug into the potato. *No one can mess up a potato*, he thought.

He was wrong.

It was tender enough, but something didn't taste quite right. Not as if it had gone bad, just that it wasn't as tasty as he remembered. He added salt and pepper, thinking that might help.

It didn't.

"Any good gossip you'd like to share?" Sam asked.

"Pretty quiet since Jenkins lit out. Ran a snake-oil salesman out of town this afternoon, though."

"Oh, that tall, lanky chap? Something-hawk?"

"Kinderhawk."

"That's the one. He tried to hawk — pardon the pun — his wares in here earlier. I chased him out with a broom. Good riddance, I say."

No one messed with Sam or her business. She'd held little regard for Dr. Jenkins, the former head of the Institute, and the feeling was mutual. He had often complained to Easton about how harmful her liquor and meat were to his patients, but Easton didn't think they were any more harmful than the ridiculous 'medicines' the man had poured down the gullets of his patients. At least Sam was honest about what she was selling.

"Well, Commander, I hope you enjoy this time on your own as much as you think you will," Sam said, pulling herself upright and tipping him a wink before heading back to the bar.

He mulled over her words in his head, trying to make sense of them. Of *course* he was going to enjoy his time alone. Ever since the brides had arrived in town, he'd barely had a minute's peace. Between his normal work load, trying to keep Matthew's wife alive, and building a life with Molly, he'd had precious little time just for himself.

Pushing the plate of disappointing food away, he carefully set his hat back on his head and shrugged into his winter coat, before tossing money on the table and heading for home. Ah, home. He hadn't really felt like calling it that for a few weeks now, but tonight it would be all his again.

Throwing open the door, he was taken aback for a split second at the cabin's cold, dark interior. *Right! Molly's not here to light the lamps.* Stamping the snow from his boots, Easton carefully stepped on a rug Molly had made from a pile of old sheets the hotel had thrown out. It made a perfect mud mat, and the knotted scraps of fabric gave the entry a warm, homey feel.

"It's got to go," he mumbled, stooping to pick up the little rug. It was just the first item that didn't belong in *his* home.

For the next half-hour, he happily collected all of Molly's things — so few, in fact, that it surprised him — and stored them in a crate, carefully placing her precious trinkets on top so they wouldn't be damaged. He slid the crate under the bed, then went about the business of putting all the furniture back where it belonged.

Only…he couldn't quite recall exactly where his small bookcase had sat. He knew which wall it should sit against, but was it near the corner or closer to the fireplace? And something about the table and chairs didn't look quite right, but he couldn't figure out what. At least he knew where his rocker belonged, because that was one item Molly hadn't rearranged.

For the better part of a month, he'd rocked quietly, reading a book or sipping a cup of tea — oftentimes both — while Molly prattled away about her day while she knitted or embroidered or whatever it was called. In the beginning, it had felt like an intrusion, but he'd learned to live with it. With her.

Easton breathed out a sigh of utter contentment when he finally leaned back in his rocking chair near the fire and breathed in the scent of his favorite English tea. Just like it used to be. He allowed his gaze to flit around his cabin, wondering why everything seemed just a little out of place, but a knock at the door startled him before he could figure it out.

Matthew stood on the doorstep, grinning like an idiot.

"What?" Easton asked perfunctorily.

"Good evening to you too! Just wanted to report that the man you wanted out of town boarded the last train of the day, and I watched it pull out. He's gone."

"Kinderhawk. Good." The man had come altogether too close to threatening Molly, and it still made Easton's blood boil.

"So…" Matthew continued, peering over Easton's shoulder, "how's everything?"

Easton huffed and rolled his eyes. "Can't a man enjoy a quiet evening alone without his coworkers coming to bother him?" The question came out a little gruffer than he'd intended.

"Yeah, I heard you were going it alone for the next week," Matthew said, poking his head inside and taking in the newly rearranged interior. "Boy, you didn't waste any time putting thing back to rights, did you? It looks as charming as a prison cell in there, as usual."

Easton looked around. Everything seemed normal to him…well, *almost* normal. He still couldn't figure out why the furniture placement didn't look right.

"What're you on about, Matthew? Looks fine to me."

Matthew shrugged. "Looks like a monk's cell to me. Then again, I like how Sinead made my cold ol' cabin into a real home." He tipped his hat and hurried off into the night.

Easton closed the door slowly, almost absent-mindedly, as he looked around the cabin with fresh eyes. What he'd always considered 'efficient' now looked stark and barren. No family photographs or heirlooms decorated the place. That required having a family in the first place. Not even a knitted afghan hung over the back of his rocker, as he'd seen in many homes he'd visited.

No wonder Molly had immediately set about making the cabin more homey. She'd grown up in a big family and had moved to a convent at a young age. He'd never stepped foot in one, but he assumed their accommodations were 'efficient' too. She'd put that life behind her to come west to marry him, and then she'd found herself in a home with just as much charm and warmth as the convent she'd fled.

Easing back into his rocker, Easton finally realized why his home didn't seem right. "Huh, whaddya know," he whispered to the roaring fire. "I miss my wife."

CHAPTER 6

"Are you *sure* you're going to be okay here all by yourself, Constance?" Molly asked Mrs. Hildebrand, who had insisted on being called by her first name.

Constance lay back on her fainting couch and waved a hand. "It's only for one night. Charles's train arrives in the morning — or is supposed to, if it doesn't get delayed again. Besides, I'm much better now that I've stopped taking all those silly potions. I really can't believe I was so gullible."

There's no shame in trusting someone who claims to be a doctor," Molly said as she packed up the small bag she'd brought with her. "I just wish your husband could be here with you."

"So do I, but Charles had a very important meeting with the board of directors this week. And between you and me, I think my moods might have been getting to him a little. I'll try to be better."

Molly laughed. "If he thinks that's bad, just wait until the baby wakes up screaming every couple of hours. He'll wish for the days when only *you* were peevish."

Though they hadn't started off on the best foot during their first meeting, Molly had grown to truly care for Constance Hildebrand. She lived in Toronto with her husband in what sounded like a mansion. They'd come to the Institute for help alleviating her normal pregnancy symptoms.

All of the woman's clothes looked too fine to even touch, much less wear, but she had no qualms about leaving them lying around her suite of rooms in piles. Over the past week, Molly had practiced her maid skills as much as she had her midwife skills.

"And you promise you won't go to the hot springs anymore, right? It's not healthy for the baby and the most it will do for you is ease your backache, which you can do just as easily with a hot water bottle."

Constance nodded. "I promise, I promise. Now will you get out of here already? I feel guilty enough as it is that I've taken you away from your new husband for so long."

Molly clenched her jaw as she slipped her mother's shawl from her shoulders so she could shrug into her coat. "I wish I knew if he felt the same. He seemed pretty eager for me to stay with you."

Constance clucked at her, then threw her legs over the side of the couch and tried to pull herself upright. Molly rushed to help her.

"No! I can do it, I just need—" she leaned backward "—a little—" then forward "—momentum." With a mighty grunt, she hauled her swollen body upright and held onto an end table until she was steady on her feet. "See?"

"Very impressive," Molly said, choking back a snicker at the display.

"Now, as I was going to say, just be patient. I see the way he looks at you, especially when he thinks you're not looking. He cares for you deeply. I must admit, I'm a little envious. It took months for Charles to look at me that way."

In such a small town, it hadn't taken long for Molly and Easton to run into each other, but their time together had always been brief and very public. As much as she'd wanted to fling herself into his arms and kiss him greedily, she was also very aware of his position in town. Plus, he certainly hadn't made the first move by so much as touching her, and it would be unseemly for a woman to be so forward in front of others, even with her own husband.

"I just wish I could make him laugh," Molly grumbled. "Just once."

Constance pulled her into a hug, or as much of one as a nine-month-pregnant woman could give. "He will, trust me. Just be patient. Commander Cooper doesn't seem the type of man who laughs easily, so when he finally does, that's when you'll know he truly trusts and loves you."

The ornate brass clock on the mantel dinged, and Molly gasped. "Oh! I meant to be home by now to make Easton breakfast. Now remember to send someone to fetch me as soon as labor pains begin, understand?"

"Yes, ma'am," Constance said, but Molly barely heard her as she sprinted out the door.

As eager as she was to see Easton, Molly spared a few minutes to poke her head into Sinead's new office at the Institute. Her friend looked every bit the competent doctor, sitting behind her desk and scribbling notes about her last patient.

"I just wanted to let you know Constance is

doing well," Molly said. "I'll check on her every day, but that baby is as stubborn as its mother."

Sinead laughed. "Or you?"

"I have no idea what you're talking about," Molly said with a prideful sniff, then gave Sinead a wink. "I'm on my way home and just wanted to let you know. Better run!"

Sinead laughed and shouted something Molly didn't hear as she ran down the hall toward the main doors, but she couldn't be bothered to stop to find out what it was. Her first priority was seeing Easton before he left for work, and if anyone tried to stop her along the way, she'd plow through them like Rocky the Reindeer plowed through snowdrifts.

Despite her eagerness — or perhaps because of it — Molly couldn't help wondering if Easton felt the same. He'd had an entire week to enjoy life without her constantly making a mess of his perfectly ordered life. Not a doubt remained that he'd done just as she'd suggested and hid every sign she ever existed. Deep down it stung a little. Her new home was so warm and comforting to her, so to know Easton thought otherwise was disappointing.

Hopefully, he wouldn't be too cranky about her putting the place back the way she liked it. As much as she wanted to please him, she also realized that she deserved to make their cabin feel like home to *her* as well. Together they could make the place suit both of them, if Easton was willing.

As Molly trudged along the snow-packed sidewalk, she made a mental note to write a long-overdue letter to Mother Superior. She'd written to her own mother three times a week since arriving, but she had yet to receive a response. A fresh wave of guilt clutched her heart in its fist, knowing she'd broken her mother's heart. What kind of daughter did that?

Molly stopped in her tracks — right in the middle of the main street — and spun a slow circle, taking in her town, her home. A light dusting of snow had fallen overnight, and it appeared no one had taken a horse or wagon thought it yet. A lone set of hoof prints marked the virgin white, and at the end stood Rocky, just staring at her.

"Good morning, Rocky," she murmured, wondering if the animal recognized her. She'd seen him around town enough that she certainly recognized *him*. The chip knocked from the tip of one prong of his antlers made it easy to distinguish him from the other reindeer that roamed through town occasionally.

Rocky snuffled, then cocked his head, as if he'd just asked a question. Molly nearly laughed at the ludicrous sight, but sobered quickly as the answer popped out of her mouth before she could stop it. "Of course I love him."

Molly gasped, while Rocky turned and trotted for the tree line.

"I love him." Full, white plumes drifted from her lips as she whispered the words she knew in her heart to be true.

"I love him," she said again, this time more loudly and with more force. As much as she loved her mother, Molly's life resided in Cougar Springs now, and regardless of whether her mother responded, Molly would continue to send her letters. She loved her mother, and that was what mattered.

"I love him!" Her shout startled a flock of mourning doves from a nearby tree and sent them darting into the slate grey sky.

Grinning like a maniac, Molly hurried through the snow as quickly as she dared. She just *had* to tell Easton. Even if he didn't say it back, she had to tell him. Her love would sustain them until he felt the same. And she knew he would, in time. God wouldn't have sent her here otherwise.

Stomping the snow off her feet as she bounded up the steps, Molly threw open the door and was faced with something she'd never expected. Instead of the sparse, bachelor cabin she'd originally arrived at, the main room looked exactly as it had when she'd left. A fire roared in the fireplace, and only a few steps away sat the table. Steaming bowls of oatmeal sat on it, with a beautiful vase filled with a fan of juniper between them. Even the trinkets her siblings had made for her were neatly organized on the mantel.

Easton stood next to the table in his civilian clothes, giving her a hesitant, lopsided smile. "Welcome home."

For a moment, Molly was so overcome by emotion she didn't know what to say. Then she flew into his arms and kissed him with all the love that was bubbling up inside her. At first, he stood stiffly in her embrace, as if he wasn't sure how to respond, then his brain shut off and his heart took over. When they finally broke apart, Molly gazed up at her husband with adoration and gratitude.

"I love you, Easton," she said, fully expecting him to withdraw from her. But something that looked awfully close to tears shimmered in his eyes.

"I love you too, Molly."

"I NEED to get ready for work," Easton said, trying to sit up, but Molly pulled him back down and snuggled into him. He was powerless to resist, so he wrapped his arms around her, tucked his nose against the top of her head, and breathed deeply. "I still can't believe you came back to me."

Molly pulled away, an adorable, crooked crease digging into her brow. "What? Why?"

He snuggled her back into the crook of his shoulder so she couldn't read his expression. The woman had a knack for knowing exactly how he felt, even if she didn't think so.

"Never mind," he murmured, loving the way she felt in his arms and wondering how he'd lived a week — really, his entire life — without her.

"Come on," she said, pulling a few of his chest hairs. "You can't say something like that and then not explain yourself. Why on earth would you think I wouldn't come home?"

"I thought I might have driven you away with… the way I am."

Molly propped herself up on an elbow and stroked her fingers lightly across his brow, easing any remaining doubt in him. "Easton, I don't love you *in spite* of the way you are. I love you *because* of the way you are. You're the calm to my crazy, and I like to think I make your life just a little more exciting."

He grinned up at her. "Boy, do you!"

Instead of grinning back, Molly dipped her head and gave him a long, lingering kiss, then nestled back into his arms and gave a sigh of utter contentment. Easton didn't have much experience in matters of the heart, so when his heart swelled at her sigh, he thought for a brief moment he might be having a heart attack. When he realized it was just the love he felt for her, he smiled and started talking.

"I was three when my mother left us."

Molly stiffened for a moment, but stayed silent, which allowed him to gather his thoughts and continue.

"I don't really remember her, but Pop spoke of her often over the next year. He loved her with everything he had and was never the same after she left. He died a year later, to the day. I was too young to understand at the time, but I put the pieces together later. The official report might say he died of accidental poisoning, but I know the truth.

Nobody puts that much rat poison in their coffee by accident and still drinks it all."

Molly gasped and made the sign of the cross, but said nothing else. His devout bride was no doubt praying for the soul of his father, and he loved her for it.

"What he really died from, though, was a broken heart. Even at the tender age of four, I knew that much. Love killed my father. It was a harsh lesson to learn so young, but it helped protect me in the orphanage."

Molly finally gazed up at him, tears making her grey eyes sparkle like sad stars. "I hate to think of you growing up in an orphanage."

He brushed away the few that fell. "Don't remember much from before, honestly. Still, I felt a bit like a paper boat bouncing around on stormy seas. You have no control over anything in your life in an orphanage. Not when or what you eat, when you go to bed, or even what you wear."

"Is that why you like things to be just so? It gives you that feeling of control you never had as a child?"

Easton had never thought of it that way before, but it made sense. "Probably."

"So you never had anything of your own either?"

"Nope."

Molly rested her cheek on his chest and cuddled him. He'd never felt more complete before in his life. What a revelation! What a joy!

"Well, I grew up in the totally opposite situation, and I still could never have something just for myself. As the oldest of fifteen, I spent my life helping to raise my siblings. All my clothes went to the next girl in line, the same with all my toys. We fought over food at the dinner table, and while we rarely went hungry, none of us ever really got our fill."

"Sounds like heaven to me." It might have been a bit of a joke, but it held a lifetime of truth. "I would have happily shared everything for the chance to have brothers and sisters and parents who loved me."

Molly's body tightened for a moment. He wasn't sure why, but it hadn't gone unnoticed by him that she'd mailed a lot of letters to her mother back in Ottawa. As far as he knew, she'd never received one back.

"I suppose," she murmured.

"Still, it must have been difficult for you to play caretaker at such a young age."

She shrugged. "It was expected. It was also expected that the oldest child of every Flynn family — that's my mother's side — go into the service of the church. There wasn't a time in my life when I wasn't told my path lay in the sisterhood. As a good Catholic and a good daughter, I never questioned my fate. But I also never truly embraced it. Secretly, on the rare occasions I found time alone, I'd daydream about being a wife and mother to my own brood. I'd pretend I was marrying an imaginary husband in front of an imaginary priest inside an imaginary church. No, not just any imaginary church. I wanted to be married in the Notre-Dame Cathedral. It's so breathtakingly beautiful, Easton. I'd love to take you there for mass someday."

"I'd like that very much, my love."

"I know Mother Superior and the sisters would love to meet you. They were all sad to see me go, but even Mother Superior could see right through me. In fact, she's the one who guided me to the path that led me to you."

"I'll be sure to send her a thank you note," he teased, kissing the top of her head and breathing in her heady scent again. Never in his life had he been happier, and there was a lifetime of these moments to look forward to.

"My mother didn't thank her, I can tell you that much. She was devastated at the news I was leaving the order before my final vows. She even refused to let me move back into the family home, despite my father's cajoling. Only by the grace of God and a gossipy organist did I learn of Miss Hazel and her plan to marry off every member of the Royal North West Mounted Police."

Easton was relieved to learn that Molly had put as little thought into their mail-order marriage as he had. But his heart broke for her at the same time. He'd been too young to remember his own mother, and still the pain cut deep. He couldn't imagine losing the woman who'd loved and raised you from birth.

"I'm sure she'll come around eventually, Molly."

"I thought so, but I don't know anymore. She is now the only one on the Flynn side whose eldest didn't follow the rules set down generations ago. I brought her great shame, and I'm not sure she'll ever forgive me. She won't even meet with Mother Superior to discuss the matter. *No one* refuses to meet with Mother Superior."

Molly sniffled against his chest, and her shoulders shook with a silent sob. Easton hooked a finger under her chin and tipped her head toward him.

"Enough of that, now," he whispered, then kissed the tip of her nose. As if they had a mind of their own, his lips moved down to hers and her whimpers turned into sighs.

She pulled back, smiling while tears still sparkled on her cheeks. "And now I know why my mother had so many babies!"

Easton barked out a surprised laugh and hugged her to him. When they separated, she gazed up at him as if she was looking at some strange, new species.

"What?" he asked.

"You laughed."

He looked around the room, as if doing so might help him make sense of what she'd said. "So?"

Molly nibbled on her lower lip, biting down a smile for some unfathomable reason. "It's a nice laugh. I like it."

"Good," he said, "because you're such bright spark of sunshine in my life, I have a feeling you're going to hear it a lot."

Their lips met again, and for the first time in his life, Easton didn't care if he was late for work.

CHAPTER 7

"What's that tune you're whistling?" Easton asked, hopping on one socked foot as he pulled a coal-black Mountie boot onto the other. They'd spent a little too much time doing their 'duty', and now he was in a hurry to make his shift at the station.

Molly laughed as she folded a towel around the lunch she'd prepared for him. "I didn't realize I *was* whistling. It's a song my mother used to sing to us at bedtime."

Her mother was never far from her mind, and hope still lingered she'd eventually come around and accept Molly's decision to live her life as she saw fit. As happy as Easton made her, Molly would always feel a pang of sadness thinking about her mother.

"Oh, that reminds me," Easton said, jamming the next foot into a boot. "A letter arrived for you yesterday. It's under the vase."

"Why didn't you tell me?" Molly dropped his lunch on the table for him to take and snatched up the letter. The beautiful vase he'd bought just for her teetered, but didn't topple, thank goodness.

Ripping into it, she held her breath, then let it out in a disappointed whoosh when she recognized her sister's handwriting. "It's from Colleen," she told him, trying to keep her voice light.

"Which one is she?" Easton asked, adjusting the brown strap across his red serge coat until it suited him.

"The next one after me. She's less than a year younger, if you can believe that."

He laughed. "Your parents *were* busy!"

Molly smiled and dipped her head to read.

Dearest Molly,

I hope this letter finds you happy and in love with your new husband. The mind boggles at what living in Cougar Springs might be like. All those rich folk prancing about, the hot springs, the magnificent scenery. Nothing at all like cold, grey, boring Ottawa, I imagine. I know it's a sin, but I truly envy you, sister dear.

Your life makes me wonder if I should contact your Miss

Hazel to find a husband of my own. Since Mother has disowned you, she has been hinting that I should take your place, so when she discovered I have been inquiring about positions as a maid all around town, she was less than pleased. I thought she would be happy that, at 26, I am finally leaving the family nest, but apparently she has other ideas. She has yet to demand it, but I am not nearly as brave as you, so if she insists I join the sisterhood, I almost certainly will not be able to resist her. You know how forceful she can be.

All is well enough in Ottawa. The boys and girls are all doing well, especially Caitlyn, who just secured a position as a secretary. She sends her love, as do all the others. Please write to me. I am desperate to hear what life in the mountains is truly like. Also, please put in a good word for me to Miss Hazel. I might require her services very soon, if things go awry.

Your favorite sister, Colleen

Molly gripped the edges of the letter so tight the paper began tearing. Her entire body vibrated with emotion she couldn't identify, but it certainly wasn't happiness. From the corner of her eye, she barely noticed Easton setting his hat on his head and turning to her.

"That's nice your sister wrote," he said.

Without warning — to him or herself — Molly

burst into tears. Great, heaving sobs wracked her body so violently she crumpled where she stood. If Easton hadn't been there to catch her, she would have fallen to the floor.

"Molly, what's wrong? Is it bad news? Did someone die?"

Easton carried her to his rocking chair and brushed the hair from her face as she tried to pull herself together. She couldn't manage coherent speech, so she shook her head and jabbed a finger into the letter. It took a few minutes for her sobs to ease into hiccups, and then she could explain.

"I-I'm sorry, Easton. I just… I didn't know…" She sniffled and gulped the bitter lump of agony down. "I didn't know they'd disowned me. I just thought she was angry."

"Disowned you? For marrying me?" Easton's eyes grew wide, then anger flickered in them.

"For leaving the convent. For not becoming a nun. But I suppose it's the same thing in the end."

Easton pulled her into a ferocious hug. "I'm so sorry, my love," he whispered in her ear. "You don't deserve that."

Molly wallowed in her misery for a moment, but it was no match for the glowing warmth of Easton's support. She might never be welcome in her childhood home again, but that didn't matter anymore. *This* was her home. Wherever Easton was, she would be home. No doubt her broken heart would take time to heal, but the solace she found in Easton's embrace would make the healing time quicker.

Brushing away her tears, she gazed up at him. "I can't tell you how much it means to me that you didn't pack away all my things while I was gone. It makes me feel like this is really, truly my home now too. It's like I've finally found my place in the world, after a lifetime of wandering around in the darkness."

Easton's eyes grew wide and all the color drained from his face. "But…I…you…um…"

The man normally played the strong, silent type to perfection, but his reaction was over the top. "What?" Molly teased.

He blinked a few times, color returning to his face full force. "You said… You told me to put it all away, remember? So I did."

At first Molly thought she misheard, but the truth of his words finally hit her like a runaway train. All the emotions that had pulsed through her since reading Colleen's letter, coupled with the blissful reunion she and Easton had just shared, overwhelmed her. Under normal circumstances, she might have felt a twinge of annoyance that he'd wiped out every memory of her existence, but that feeling was amplified tenfold after such a tumultuous morning. With no warning at all, the rage consumed her to the point of blindness.

Shoving Easton away, she leapt to her feet and spun on him. "What, did you just put it all back the way it was to fool me into thinking you liked having me here?"

Easton stumbled, but quickly regained his footing. She jerked away when he tried reaching for her.

"No, Molly. That wasn't it at all."

"I don't believe you!" she shouted, stomping past him to their — *his* — room and yanking her bag from under the bed. "You couldn't *wait* for me to leave so everything could go back to the way it was before."

Easton tried to stop her from shoving her few pieces of clothing into the bag, but she pulled out of his reach. "Molly, listen—"

"No, you listen! You lied to me." He tried to break in with an objection, but she cut him off. "Not with your words, but definitely with your actions. You spent the entire week enjoying having me gone, enjoying having everything the way *you* like it. I know, because why else wouldn't you have tried to see me more while I was with Constance?"

He stood, gape-mouthed, just watching her. Molly huffed.

"That's what I thought. Now move!"

She shoved past him again, ignoring the way her body reacted at being in such close proximity to him, and headed for the door.

"Where are you going?" he finally asked, frustration tinging his words.

"Somewhere where I'm appreciated." She flung open the door with great relish, only to find big, fat fluffy snowflakes falling steadily. She'd hoped to storm out and slam the door behind her, but even in her blinding rage, she wasn't about to go out without her coat. Just as she reached for it, though, Easton slammed the door on her heart.

"Where's that? I thought you didn't have anywhere else to go and that's why you had to marry me."

Molly's heart stopped and she let her bag slip from her fingers in shock. If her blood hadn't been pumping so furiously through her veins, she surely would have dropped dead right there in the doorway. But she didn't. Instead, she bolted outside without so much as a glance back. Somewhere behind her, through the whoosh of her racing heart and sound of her sobs, Easton's shout filtered through.

"Molly, come back! The weather's turning bad!"

So's our marriage, she thought as she ran blindly into the falling snow.

※

As Molly's fast-moving form disappeared into the thickening snow, Easton started after her. After a few steps he stopped and looked to the sky. Judging from the dark cloud mass pushing across the mountain, the weather was only going to get worse before it got any better. Maybe a whole lot worse.

A snowstorm hadn't been predicted the day before, but the weather changed quickly in the mountains, especially in the winter, and he hadn't been into the office yet. Surely Nathaniel or Samuel would have reported to him this morning if a storm had been in the day's forecast, which meant this would hit the entire town by surprise.

He tried to catch Molly's silhouette through the snow, but she was gone. She shouldn't be out in the snow without a coat, but he tried to comfort himself with the fact she'd been heading toward the hotel.

No doubt she'd hide out in Mrs. Hildebrand's room for the duration of the storm. She'd be chilled to the bone by the time she got there, but at least she'd be safe.

Now he just needed to make sure the rest of the town was too.

When he arrived at the station, all three of his men stood outside watching the snow coming down harder and harder.

"Nice of you to join us, Commander," Matthew teased, though Easton heard very little humor in his tone. "We were just about to send out a search party."

Ignoring him, Easton walked straight into the office. "Where's today's forecast?"

Samuel handed it to him. "Calls for cloudy skies, that's all. If it had said a storm was coming, I would have fetched you right away."

"And the next one won't come in till late tonight," Easton said, going to the town map hanging on the wall. "If this is as big as I think it's going to be, we can't wait for that forecast before battening down the town."

"Agreed," Nathaniel said. "Where do you want us to start? Normally, we have time to get to everyone before the storm starts, but the way it's coming down, we'll top a foot pretty quickly."

"Yeah, boss," Matthew added. "No way will we be able to warn the folks on the outskirts *and* our quadrant before the road becomes impassable."

One of the first things Easton had done as Commander was to assign each Mountie approximately one-quarter of the town itself in the event of emergencies. They all patrolled the entire town, but when a storm threatened, each man was responsible for making sure everyone in his quadrant was safe, accounted for and ready for the bad weather.

Easton sucked on his teeth as he studied the map. There were at least fifteen or so families scattered around outside of town, in pretty much every direction. Any way he looked at it, he couldn't figure out a way to reach the families without sacrificing the safety of hundreds in town — not to mention his own men.

"If only we had telephones up here," Samuel mused.

"Well, we don't," Easton said a little more sharply than he meant. "We'll just have to hope and pray they're all smart enough to see the signs and prepare themselves."

Sleep would elude him until he knew each and every one of those families was safe. In the meantime, he'd do everything in his power to make sure the rest of the town was too.

"Okay, we'll go door-to-door in our quadrants to this point." He pointed to just past the edge of town, an area that encompassed nearly all of the local population. "We'll rendezvous back here in two hours, at four o'clock. Remember protocol?"

Matthew sighed, as if he'd heard it a thousand times — probably because he had. "If we don't check in or send word by four-thirty, a search party will be formed, and there's nothing more embarrassing to a Mountie than having to be rescued by a bunch of locals."

"And?" Easton prompted.

"And," Samuel answered, "that man will have to sing 'O Canada' as loud as he can on the steps of the Institute every morning for an entire month."

"Right. So be safe and don't get yourselves lost out there."

As Easton made his way through his quadrant, reminding folks to bring in their children, pets, horses, or anything else they didn't want to get frozen and buried in snow, his mind never strayed far from Molly. He itched to stop at the Institute first to make sure she was okay, but he always saved the hotel for last because it took so much time. Most guests were somewhere on-site anyway.

So he did his duty — his mind flashed to Molly snuggling with him in bed whenever he heard the word 'duty' anymore — and made his way through town. Second-to-last stop: Sam's Saloon.

Only one patron stood at the bar nursing a half-empty beer mug when Easton strolled in, brushing the snow from his coat and hat at the entrance. Sam was nowhere in sight.

"Looks like a storm's coming, Sam," he called toward the bar.

The woman popped her head up, caught sight of him and stood. "Afternoon, Commander. What was that now?"

"Unforecasted storm coming in," he said as he tapped the brooding beer-drinker on the shoulder. When the man turned cloudy eyes on him, Easton said, "You better get home while you still can, sir. Where do you live?"

The man blinked slowly, a sure sign he was inebriated. "Just over at the Institute." Only, it came out sounding like, *Juss over t'Inshtitoo.*

"Oh boy," Easton mumbled, shooting Sam a scolding glance. She shrugged in response. "Gonna have to ask you to close up shop until it passes, I'm afraid. Don't want to tempt anyone to risk their lives for a drink."

"I understand," Sam said with a sigh and threw a dishtowel on the bar. "It must be a bad one, huh?"

"No idea. Wasn't forecast. Why?"

Sam narrowed her eyes as she assessed him. "Because you look like half the town is already dead, Commander."

"Sir," Easton said to the customer, "why don't you go get your coat and scarf on, and I'll escort you to the hotel. It's my last stop anyway."

The man gave a wobbly nod, and as soon as he teetered off, Easton told Sam all about the morning's argument with Molly. "One minute, everything was peaches and cream, the next she was yelling at me for something *she* told me to do!"

Sam threw her head back, her cackle echoing through the empty saloon. "You know how I said you should put yourself in her shoes?"

Easton nodded.

"Well, sometimes you can do everything right and we'll still want to hit you in the head with a skillet. Women's emotions can come out in strange ways."

Sam might as well have been speaking a foreign language. He felt utterly, hopelessly lost. "Don't know what any of that means."

She smiled and reached across the bar to pat him on the shoulder. "I know, honey. Just keep the faith. She'll be back. That gal looks at you like you're the ice in her whiskey. She ain't going anywhere."

"You comin', Mountie?" the drunk man called as he waited by the door, swaying gently.

Easton looked deep in Sam's eyes, hoping the answer — an answer he could understand, anyway — lay there, but all he saw was amusement. Shaking his head, he tipped his hat to her and headed for the door. Whatever she meant, Easton wouldn't relax until he saw Molly again.

CHAPTER 8

"Better get inside, miss," said a young hotel porter as Molly labored through the deepening snow.

"It sure is coming down," she said, smiling at him with gratitude, though her heart was still on fire from her argument with her husband. "It was just a dusting this morning."

The young man looked to the darkening sky and shook his head. "Looks like a whopper, you ask me."

Molly stood in front of the roaring fire in the hotel's lobby to warm up before she headed up to Constance's suite. As the feeling returned to her wet, frozen toes and fingers, she cursed herself for not grabbing her coat as she stormed out of the cabin, but she'd just been so angry.

The warmer Molly became, the cooler her temper grew. The heat from her anger had kept her going until she reached the hotel, but now the gravity of the situation sat heavy on her heart. With each draft of cold air that trickled in from outside and chilled her warming skin, a dagger of icy shame stabbed her soul.

She'd behaved like a spoiled child when Easton had told her the truth. He could have just as easily lied and pretended he had indeed left the place exactly as-is, but he'd trusted her with his honesty. And just look at how she'd betrayed that trust.

One glance out the big picture window told Molly she wasn't going anywhere until the snow died down, which hurt her heart even more. All she wanted to do — now that she wasn't consumed by her own self-pity — was to run back into Easton's arms and beg his forgiveness for behaving like a brat.

With a deep, bracing breath, she pulled herself from the comfort of the fire and ascended the magnificent grand staircase until she reached the top floor of the Institute. This floor, she'd learned, was reserved for the most wealthy clients, as it afforded the best views and was comprised solely of suites. The medical section of the Institute sat on the opposite side of the sprawling complex.

With each step, Molly's pain lightened just a little. The thought of talking with Constance about her fight with Easton would help, no doubt about it. Constance had been married for ten years, and had given Molly quite a lot of sound advice already. Of course, it went both ways, since Molly had advised Constance on many aspects of pregnancy, birth and caring for her baby. What had started out as an adversarial relationship had blossomed into a true and sincere friendship.

Molly rapped on Constance's door, hoping she wouldn't wake her from a nap. She waited patiently because she knew exactly how difficult it was for a heavily pregnant woman to get up from a chair. If she'd been lying down, the time would double or even triple.

After a couple of minutes, she knocked again, this time harder, thinking the first time hadn't been loud enough to wake her friend. Still nothing. Not even a rustle from behind the heavy wooden door. Molly pressed her ear up against it to listen for signs of movement from inside, but the door gave way from the pressure.

"Oh!" she squeaked, surprised that Constance

had not only left the door unlocked, but ajar. "Constance?"

Molly closed the door softly behind her. A shiver rippled across her skin at the chill in the room. The fireplace showed no signs of embers, which meant it hadn't been lit in hours. Alarm bells clanged in her head, but she did her best to tune them out as she looked around the place.

"Constance! It's Molly!"

Nothing seemed out of place. The coat rack stood next to the door, as usual. The magazines were splayed in a perfect fan on the coffee table. The roses in the vase on the dining table looked fresh.

Only…nothing moved. Not even the soft rustle of a bedsheets could be heard. Only the quiet patter of snow against the window and the sounds of her own feet on the plush carpet gave Molly any confidence she hadn't lost her sense of hearing.

Frosty tendrils of dread wound their way through her gut as she searched every room, but no Constance. Standing in the doorway of the master bedroom, Molly took in the rumpled bed linens, the drawn curtains, the book lying on the floor. Panic tried to catch hold, but she pounded it down by telling herself her friend must be somewhere in the hotel. Or maybe with a doctor.

Then it hit her. "Oh, maybe she's in the medical wing giving birth!"

Hope brushed aside any remaining fear as she rushed for the door. Some tiny tickle at the back of her brain tried to come forward, but she had more important things to think about. As much as she regretted arguing with Easton, at least it led to her being in the Institute before Constance gave birth. Too much longer and no one would have been able to fetch her.

Shoving her way through the doors to the medical wing, Molly rushed up to the nurses' station so out of breath it took a moment for her to speak clearly. The nurse waited patiently.

"Constance…Hildebrand," Molly finally managed between gasps for air.

The nurse consulted a list, then shook her head. "I don't see her name."

"She's having a baby?" That sense of unease leaked back into Molly's heart.

"Hmm, let me check again." A deep furrow creased the nurse's brow. "No, I'm sorry. She hasn't been checked in."

"No, she has to be. Please check again."

"Miss—"

"*Please!*"

The woman sighed and double-checked her list, finally shaking her head again. "I'm sorry. She hasn't been admitted."

Connections Molly's brain hadn't made earlier finally clicked into place. The coat rack by the door had been empty, and Constance's bedside table, which had been cluttered with half-empty bottles of various elixirs, had also been cleared.

Then it hit her like a lightning bolt. How had she missed it? How had she forgotten?

Her mother's shawl. She'd taken it off before leaving Constance that morning so she could put on her coat. Her eagerness to see Easton had apparently overpowered her memory because she realized she hadn't packed it. Yet it had been nowhere in the suites or she would have noticed it. That meant only one thing: Constance had it…wherever she was.

Molly took ten steps to leave the medical wing, but she was already out of breath by the time she passed through the door. Real, justified panic gripped her, which was why she didn't look where she was going and smacked face-first into a towering wall of red.

"Oof!" a masculine voice she'd recognize anywhere coughed.

"Easton!" she cried. Easton would know what to do!

"Molly? What are you doing down here? Never-mind that. Molly, I'm so sorry for—"

Molly shook her head frantically and waved away his unwarranted apology. "No, I'm sorry. I let my temper get the better of me again. But we don't have time for all that right now."

His brow furrowed, and that look of genuine concern cemented Molly's love for him. "Why? What's wrong?"

"It's Constance. She's not in her room, and she hasn't been checked into the medical wing. Something's wrong."

Easton rubbed her arms, which soothed her more than she'd thought possible. "She's probably somewhere in the hotel. Don't worry."

"No, I have a bad feeling, Easton. Her coat was gone, and she took my shawl with her. *And* her bottles of that snake-oil elixir are gone."

Easton dug a finger under his hat to scratch his head. "So?"

"So?" Molly asked, incredulous.

No, stay calm. Constance needs you.

Taking a deep breath, Molly explained. "She bundled up to go outside in the cold, Easton. And even if she doesn't think the elixir will do her any good, there's so much alcohol in it, she probably thinks it will keep her warm, wherever she's going."

"And where do you think she's going?"

Molly chewed her lip. "No idea."

Easton took less than three seconds to make a decision. "Okay, then. I need to make sure everyone is accounted for in the hotel, so we'll form a team and take it floor by floor. If we don't find her…"

He let the words die on his lips. Molly only hoped Constance wouldn't die before they found her.

※

After an hour of searching every room in the hotel, as well as confirming with the medical ward's staff, Mrs. Hildebrand was nowhere to be found. The hotel manager, Mr. Jackson, had accompanied Easton on the search, and along the way they ticked off every other guest registered at the hotel.

"I wonder where she could be," Jackson pondered, looking far less worried than Easton felt. The man had soft hands and a soft conscious.

"And your staff triple-checked the hot springs?"

"I sent my two most trusted men," Jackson confirmed. "They searched every pool, and dressing room, even the outhouse. Nothing."

Easton's belly cramped. The snow was no longer falling thick and soft. Wind had spooled up, and the white fluffs from earlier had turned into stinging nettles. If Mrs. Hildebrand was out there, wandering around lost…

"I think I know where she went," Molly called, skipping down the stairs so fast Easton's heart leapt in his throat. She didn't look happy, exactly. More determined than anything.

"Where?" Easton rushed over to her, just in case she tripped and she went tumbling. But she didn't. She bounded down to the second-to-last step and stopped so she wouldn't have to crane her neck to look up at him. She set down a satchel next to her feet so she could button up her coat and wrap a big red scarf around her neck.

"The Secret Springs."

Easton frowned. He and his men knew about what the locals called the Secret Springs, nestled in the forest not far from the Institute. Few bothered with them since the Institute's springs had such comfortable accommodations, but some of the locals refused to pay a fee to enjoy them, preferring to follow a faint, ungroomed trail through the trees to a natural upwelling in the rocks. It wasn't a particularly difficult trek, but a mother-to-be making that hike seemed impossible.

"No," he said flatly. "She'd never make the Secret Springs."

"And that's exactly why we have to go find her," Molly argued.

"What makes you think that's where she went, anyway?"

"Some porter told her their waters were the most powerful, and she's desperate to have that baby. I *know* that's where she went, Easton. It's the only thing that makes any sense."

Determination and conviction glinted in her steel-grey eyes. Easton still wasn't convinced, though he had no other ideas of where else Mrs. Hildebrand could have gone.

Normally, he would have organized a full search party, but with the weather deteriorating so quickly, it was far too risky. Of course his men were out warning the rest of the town, and it would take too long to hunt them down to help. By the time he rounded them all up, dark would have fallen. The only thing worse than searching for a missing person in a snowstorm was searching for a missing person in a snowstorm *at night*. As it was, he'd just barely have enough light to make it to the Secret Springs and back without the burden of assisting a hopefully uninjured pregnant woman.

"Fine," he said, whipping his hat off and running a hand across the top of his head. "But you're staying here, where I know you're safe."

Molly gave him a look like he was the class dunce. "Don't be ridiculous, Easton. What if she's in distress? Or, the good Lord forbid, giving birth in the middle of the snow? Do you know how to deliver a baby? What if something goes wrong?"

Easton felt the grimace, but was powerless to stop it. Mounties learned about hunting down villains and bringing them to justice, not birthing babies. "Um..."

"Exactly!" Molly sniffed, then covered her head with the scarf and snatched up her bag. "I have everything I need in here, thanks to Sinead setting me up with everything in case of an emergency. And I'd say this is an emergency, wouldn't you?"

He stumbled on what to say, but when Jackson snickered at the exchange, Easton shot him a hard glare. "Enough of that, now."

Turning back to Molly, vaguely aware of

Jackson scurrying away, he said, "Fine. But you stick close to me, and if she's not there, we high-tail it back, agreed?"

"But—"

"Agreed?" he demanded more firmly. "If not, we can sit here and cuddle by the roaring fire."

Molly rolled her eyes. "Agreed."

THE MOMENT they entered the tree line, the piercing, painful wind calmed some, allowing them to talk. Easton went first.

"Molly, I'm so sorry for what I said. I didn't mean for it to come out the way it sounded."

Molly, tromping ahead of him, her long red skirt caked with snow up to her knees, shook her head. "Yes you did, and that's okay. I'm sure a part of you wonders if I only stayed because I have nowhere else to go."

He hadn't, until that very moment. When she said it, he realized that's exactly what he'd wondered. "I…"

Molly glanced over her shoulder and smiled. "I'd stop right now and show you just how much I honestly and truly love you, Easton Cooper, but we have more important things to do at the moment. I hope you'll believe me when I tell you there is *always* someplace else to go — a friend's house, a church, a tent in the woods — but there is absolutely no place I'd rather be than with you."

Easton let go of that nagging insecurity he hadn't even been consciously aware of and felt it float away like a helium balloon on the wind. It was almost as if the last puzzle piece of his heart locked into place, and now he was whole.

"Besides, I'm the one who should be apologizing," Molly said, her breath coming out in steamy rushes, only to be broken apart by the breeze. "The news my parents actually disowned me hurt me deeply, and I suppose I lashed out at you to make someone else feel as badly as I did. I'm so sorry."

Her voice had become smaller and smaller until the last words were just a squeak. Despite the urgent nature of their mission, Easton grabbed her arm and whirled her around to face him. Tears pooled in her eyes, so Easton kissed them away.

"I will be your sounding board any time you need one, my love," he said, salt tickling his tongue. "As long as we can talk things through and go on loving each other."

A single sob shook Molly's shaking frame, and

she dropped her head in a nod. With a sniffle, she met his eyes. "Now let's go find Constance."

ON A FINE DAY, the easy hike to the Secret Springs would have taken ten minutes, but in the storm it took closer to thirty. Gloom had already settled into the nooks and crannies of the forest, but at least there was enough light to see the path ahead. Easton had borrowed a new-fangled flashlight from the manager before leaving the hotel, but who knew how much life was left in it. He wanted to save it until he really needed it.

"I think I see it!" Molly shouted, and sped up as much as she could in the snow, which grew deeper with each passing minute. When she rounded a bend and disappeared from sight, his heart thumped triple-time, even though he knew she was only a few feet ahead of him.

Rounding the corner, Easton saw Molly standing over the rocky pool, her shoulders slumped. Even from a distance, he saw no sign of Mrs. Hildebrand, just some litter an inconsiderate visitor had left behind. He wrapped his arm around his wife's shivering shoulders and gave her a reassuring half-hug.

"See? She's not here either. She must be in town, or she found some hidey-hole in the hotel we didn't find. Let's get back before—"

"No." Molly stooped and grabbed the litter. "This is one of the elixirs she'd been taking to bring on labor. She promised not to take them anymore. She also promised not to go to the hot springs anymore, but look…" She touched one of the rocks surrounding the pool and held up her hand. "It's still wet, not frozen. She's been here, Easton, and she couldn't have gone very far."

She certainly hadn't gone back the way they'd come, and there was no other path to the hotel, that he knew of.

"There!" Molly shouted and bounded through the snow drifts. "Tracks lead this way!"

Easton ran after her, not bothering trying to stop her. He wasn't about to risk Molly's life searching for too much longer, but he also had a duty to do whatever he could to find Mrs. Hildebrand. Ten more minutes, and then he'd insist on turning back. Even then, he'd have to use the flashlight by the end.

They had barely tracked the footsteps for five minutes before they disappeared. The snow had partially filled them in, but the darkness and the blinding snow made them impossible to see.

"Constance!" Molly cried, her voice barely rising above the level of the shrieking wind. "Constance!"

"Molly," he said gently, pulling her to him. Her entire body shook violently from the cold, one of the first signs of hypothermia. "That's it. We're turning back."

Molly broke free and screamed, "No! She's out there, Easton! We have to find her!"

"I'm sorry, Molly, but we'll be lucky if *we* make it back alive, and that's only if we go back now."

Molly screamed for her friend a few more times, frantic to find her. Easton sighed and flicked on the flashlight. He was momentarily blinded by the wall of white light reflecting off the snow, but his eyes quickly adjusted. The beam barely reached ten feet in front of them, and then it started flickering. He moved to switch it off to save the batteries when Molly pointed ahead of them.

"There! Shine it over there!"

He saw nothing at first, but a second pass revealed a patch of red showing through a blanket of white. Molly dug it out and whooped in triumph.

"It's my mother's shawl! She has to be up ahead, Easton. Please, just a little farther."

He wanted to say no, that it was time, but a movement off to the side caught his eye. The reindeer Molly called Rocky trotted past at a quick clip. He stopped and stared straight into the beam of light, then turned and continued into the darkness. On a hunch, Easton followed the animal's track.

Within a minute, a dark, looming shape appeared at the edge of the circle of light. His breath caught in disbelief. Two more steps confirmed his suspicion. It was a small, dilapidated shack, probably built by some unknown hunter or trapper ages ago. And the door stood open.

CHAPTER 9

At Easton's shout of surprise, Molly dragged her eyes from where she was stepping to the structure illuminated by his fancy electric light.

"Constance!"

They ran together, blinded by the near-whiteout conditions. Molly had never been more cold in her life, but she barely felt her frozen toes anymore. All that mattered was finding Constance.

Easton bolted through the open door first, and just as she was about to rush in, Molly caught a glimpse of Rocky standing in the lee of the little shack, watching her. His coat was tipped with white clumps, but he looked otherwise unperturbed. She blew him a kiss.

"Stay safe, my friend," she muttered, then closed the door behind her.

Wind shrieked around the cabin. A few loose boards rattled and allowed frigid air, along with a smattering of snow, to blow in. Easton knelt over the crumpled form of Constance Hildebrand, lying motionless on the floor. For the briefest of moments, Molly thought they were too late. But then Constance let out the sweetest, most blood-curdling scream Molly had ever heard.

"Constance, it's Molly and Easton," she said, rushing to her friend's side as she writhed on the floor.

"Molly! It hurts!"

"I know, honey, I know. I want you to hold my hand and take a few deep breaths for me." Turning to Easton, who looked absolutely petrified, she said quietly, "First, start the biggest fire you can build. Second, find something to melt snow in. Third, seal up that gap over there so we can get warm."

He stood, although he looked a bit shaky, and nodded, giving Constance one last, mystified look. Then he set to work.

"Molly," Constance said through gritted teeth, "where am I?"

The world around Molly disappeared, and the warmth of confidence that came with experience calmed her nerves. She smiled and brushed a dead leaf from Constance's forehead.

"I have no idea, actually. We followed your tracks from the Secret Springs to here, but it's too dark outside to know where we are exactly. All I know is I'm glad you found this place, Constance. Now breathe with me."

After the contraction passed, Molly and Easton moved Constance closer to the weak fire. Molly crumpled her shawl and placed it under Constance's head. Soon the fire would be roaring and they might have to move her farther away, but for now they all needed to warm up.

"What happened, Constance? Why did you come up here?"

Tears spilled freely from the woman's deep brown eyes. "I'm sorry," she whispered weakly. Molly didn't like the sound of that at all. "I'm just so tired. I know I promised not to, but I…I'm just so tired."

Constance's eyelids drooped and her voice trailed off. Molly felt for her, and had no doubt the woman was exhausted from her misadventure, but now wasn't the time for a nap. Molly shook her shoulders gently, rousing her.

"Tell me what happened, every detail, while I check you and your baby, okay?"

"Okay," Constance whimpered. But the moment Molly threw the woman's skirt over her knees, she snapped awake. "Oh! But there's a man in the room!"

"I won't look, ma'am," Easton said from the corner, where he was stuffing an old gunny sack in the hole.

"If it wasn't for Easton, we never would have found you. He not only saved your life, but your baby's too. Isn't that wonderful?"

"Y-yes, I suppose," Constance replied hesitantly. Another wave of pain gripped her, and any objection to Easton's presence flew out with the last draft of cold.

Molly said a quick prayer and crossed herself before examining Constance. The Lord had been watching over her friend, that much was certain. Aside from being cold, Constance was fine. The baby was positioned correctly, but she wouldn't know much more until the little bundle of joy made an appearance.

"You're doing great, Constance. Those contractions were just a few minutes apart, so I think your baby's almost here. Just keep taking nice calming breaths, and tell me what happened."

Constance explained, through her breathing and a couple more contractions, that she'd become bored and impatient after Molly left that morning. Her back had been aching all night, and all she could think about was soaking in the hot springs, but she hadn't wanted to risk Molly catching her using the Institute's pools. She'd promised not to, after all. She'd heard about the Secret Springs, and how they were rumored to have even more magical powers because they were the source for the Institute's springs. The forecast didn't call for any more snow, and she'd thought the walk would help start labor.

"What about the elixir?" Molly asked, trying to keep any note of accusation out of her voice.

"I'd been using it for weeks, so I didn't think one more dose would hurt," Constance whined defensively.

"Okay, then what?"

"I guess I fell asleep. I only woke up because my head dipped underwater."

Molly couldn't hold back her gasp of shock or a flare of righteous anger. "I told you that elixir was nothing but dressed-up alcohol! You could have drowned!"

Constance began crying, and once again, Molly chided herself for speaking before thinking. Hugging her friend, Molly cooed, "It's okay, I'm sorry. You're fine, you're fine."

Only when Constance was calm again did Molly press for more information.

"Once I woke up, I climbed out of the pool and got dressed. My entire body was redder than the lobsters my family eats at Christmas. Do you think I boiled my baby, Molly?"

Molly almost laughed, but the sheer terror in Constance's eyes stopped her. "No, your baby's fine. If *you* didn't get boiled alive, your baby didn't. What did you do after you dressed?"

Molly honestly wanted to know, but part of the exercise was to distract Constance, to keep her talking and awake.

"I had my first contraction. I've never known such pain before. I sat on a log for a very long time, wondering what to do. The snow had started while I was asleep and covered my tracks. But I had no intention of giving birth out in the middle of the forest, all alone, so I waited till the pain had eased and I set out. I guess I got turned around, though. I thought I knew where I was going, but it didn't take long before I realized my mistake. I'm not ashamed to say I was scared, Molly."

"I bet."

"Oh! Here comes another!"

That contraction came even sooner than the last, which meant Constance was close, but not quite ready. She caught her breath and continued the story, as if she needed to get it all out before concentrating on bringing her child into the world.

"I started crying — panicking, actually. I turned to follow my tracks back and see if I could figure out where I went wrong when a huge beast burst out of the woods."

"What was it?" Molly asked, breathless with fear for her friend.

"A reindeer, of all things. It jumped out at me, gave me the fright of my life, then sauntered away. He kept stopping and looking over his shoulder at me, like he wanted me to follow him."

Molly caught Easton's gaze. *Rocky.*

"I swear it's true!" Constance must have seen the exchange and misunderstood the meaning. "And he led me right here to this cabin. By then, the contractions were coming pretty quickly. I just barely made it into the cabin before collapsing."

Sobs shook her shoulders and Molly pulled her into her arms. "Shh, no tears. This is a happy day. The happiest. You get to meet your baby!"

Constance's sobs turned to moans, then screams. "It's coming!"

Molly lost track of time as she tended to Constance. Easton crouched at her head, speaking to her in low, soothing tones as Molly worked. Once he even grimaced in pain when Constance gripped his hand too hard. Molly wanted to tell him he had no idea what pain was, but then again, neither did she.

She hoped to one day, though. And many times.

෴

AFTER WHAT SEEMED LIKE AN ETERNITY, the screaming stopped, replaced with quiet sobs of exhaustion, and then an ear-piercing squall. Easton wanted to slap his hands to his ears, but Molly motioned for the shawl under Mrs. Hildebrand's head. The poor woman barely registered that he removed her pillow, but as soon as Molly brought the baby girl — swaddled in the shawl — to her, she perked up and smiled in wonder at the tiny life she'd created.

Easton took that as his cue to leave and moved to a rickety crate on the opposite side of the far-too-small shack. He averted his eyes, not wanting to witness private women's business. Still, the process had fascinated him.

For the first time in his life, he wondered why everyone treated women like they were such fragile creatures. This woman had not only trekked through a snowstorm while she was in labor, but she suffered through what sounded like unimaginable pain, only to smile at the end.

He'd thought the same about Molly, that she needed to be protected and sheltered. Yet she'd pressed on long after he'd been ready to turn around.

Men could learn a lot about bravery from women, he thought.

"Are you okay?" Molly asked, sitting on another rickety crate and slipping her hand into his.

He squeezed it and jerked his head toward mother and child. "I'm not sure. Are they?"

Molly chuckled. "They're right as rain. I'm not sure they would have been if we hadn't found them, though. She was very cold and very frightened."

"So was I, to be honest." Easton looked deep into her eyes, trying to convey something he was having trouble articulating. "But I've never been more terrified than when you ran out of the house this afternoon."

A pained look flashed in Molly's eyes, echoing the flicker of the fire behind them. "I apologized—"

"I know, and I accepted it. I did. It's just that I've been the one who usually runs away from our…disagreements, so when you ran out, I really didn't know if you'd be coming back."

Molly scooched her crate closer and kissed his cheek. "I told, you, I'm not going anywhere. This is my life. *You* are my life."

He already knew it, deep down, but it comforted him to hear it again. "As you are mine."

He gave her a lingering kiss that drew a sigh from her. She leaned her head on his shoulder and sighed again.

"I don't think I've ever felt so happy. As much as I want my parents to accept me, helping Constance has made me realize I don't need their approval to live a happy life. Being with you makes me happy. Helping mothers and delivering babies makes me happy. Living in our little cabin with hardly any possessions makes me happy."

Easton grinned and kissed her forehead. "Now *I've* never been so happy!"

The wind howled hard enough to blow dogs off their chains outside, but the three of them — no, *four* — were safe and warm, thanks to Molly's persistence. He made a mental note to send Miss Hazel a thank you note. What a sad, lonely life he'd led before Molly exploded on the scene.

"I want lots of those, you know," she said, peering up at him.

"Hmm? Lots of what?"

Molly jerked her head back toward Constance and her slumbering baby. "I come from a big family, and I want a big family of my own…with you."

Doubt doused his contented mood. It would have been a lie for him to say he'd never thought about it, but those thoughts had always ended the same way.

"I don't know, Molly. I've never really had a family. I barely remember my father. I don't think I'll know how to do it."

Molly snaked an arm through his and hugged it tightly. "That's okay, I'll show you how it's done. And I really think it'll come naturally for you. You're kind and caring and loyal. You'll make a great dad, Easton."

Her faith in him gave him hope. "You think?"

She gazed up at him, unabashed love pouring from her eyes. "I know." She glanced over at her patients, then up at him again. "In fact, they'll probably sleep for hours. Why don't we get started right now?"

Easton smiled at first, then laughed when her hand slipped inside his coat. He pulled it out and held her to him, simply enjoying their closeness. "Enough of that, now," he whispered.

But deep down Easton knew he'd never get enough of his beautiful, wild bride.

EPILOGUE

"Wake up, sleepyhead."

Molly's sweet voice whispered into Easton's consciousness as he rose up from the depths of sleep. He squinted against the cool light shimmering through a frost-covered window. Molly stood next to the bed, gently trying to rouse him. Stretching his arms wide, he yawned loudly, then clamped her into a surprise bear hug and pulled her on top of him. Her giggles were the perfect way to start off their first Christmas together.

"Stop it, you brute," she laughed, slapping his chest and getting back to her feet. She jammed her hands onto her hips and gave him a mock glare. "It's time to do your duty."

Easton waggled his eyebrows at her suggestively. "That sounds like the perfect way to start the day."

"Not *those* duties, and you know it. The sooner you finish, the sooner our Christmas can start. And I'm planning a feast you'll never forget."

"Mmm, can't wait. Any hints?" he asked as whipped back the covers.

Brr! Instead of dressing in the chilly bedroom, he grabbed his uniform and followed Molly out so he could dress by the fire. Technically, his task didn't require him to be in uniform, but it seemed only fitting.

"Did I forget to tell you? Constance's husband sent away for lobsters, as is their family custom, and he ordered extras for us. Isn't that thoughtful?"

"Very," he said tugging on a thick wool sock, grateful for Molly's own thoughtfulness at setting them in front of the fire to warm. "Have you ever had lobster?"

Molly made a face. "No, is it strange? They certainly *look* strange. They remind me of giant versions of the crayfish my little brothers love to catch back home."

Easton smiled. "That's more or less exactly what they are. Just bigger. They're delicious."

"They better be, because cooking them is going to be scary," Molly said with a laugh, pouring him a steaming cup of his favorite English tea.

"I'll be here to protect you. Speaking of, how are Mrs. Hildebrand and baby Molly?"

A flush of pride filled his wife's face. "Beautifully. They've decided to stay through the New Year to allow her to recuperate. I still can't believe they named her after me."

"Really?" he asked as he buttoned up his red serge coat. "I would have been more surprised if they hadn't, considering it was you who saved both their lives that night."

"I seem to recall a handsome Mountie being there too," she said.

"True, but only a crazy person would name their daughter Easton."

Molly laughed at his little joke as if it was the funniest thing she'd ever heard. He loved her laugh, and he especially loved making her laugh. And he loved her for laughing at his jokes that weren't really all *that* funny. It made him feel loved.

"Yesterday she gave me the gloves she'd accused me of stealing. She said it was the only way to repent, and she wouldn't let me refuse. Isn't that thoughtful?"

Easton said nothing. Sitting in his rocker, he motioned for Molly to sit in the one he'd had built for her as an early Christmas present. She blinked in puzzlement, but sat without comment.

"I want to give you something too." He reached into his pocket, and Molly gasped.

"But you've already given me this beautiful chair," she protested. "I don't need anything more, Easton."

He pulled a folded envelope from his pocket and held it out to her. "It's not from me. It came in yesterday, but I was too busy to bring it to you. When I got home last night, you were fast asleep, and I didn't want to wake you."

Molly frowned and took the envelope. Her eyes grew wide at the writing on the front, and Easton knew he'd guessed right. His heart raced, hoping its contents didn't ruin her day, but the very fact her mother had written at all was a good sign the rift between them was healing.

Tears dripped onto the letter as she read, making the ink blur, but she kept on. With her head dropped and her flaming red hair covering most of her face, he couldn't tell if they were happy tears or sad tears. He prayed for happy. Finally, she tipped her face up to him, a beatific smile radiating from the inside out.

"Good news?" he asked hopefully.

She pressed her lips together to stop from crying and nodded mutely, then launched herself into his arms. He let her weep for a few moments before easing her back.

"You can tell me about it over breakfast," he said. "Right now I need get going."

Molly sniffled and nodded. "But before you go, I want to give you something too."

She pulled a small brown paper package from the basket she used to hold her yarn, and laid it in his hand. It was so small. And smooshy. He caught her eye and smiled.

"What is it?"

"Only one way to find out," she teased, wiping the remaining tears from her cheeks.

Easton couldn't remember ever receiving a present before. Not like this. Sometimes grateful locals would drop off fresh-baked bread or cookies, but as much as he appreciated the gesture, it wasn't the same.

Slowly and with great care, he pulled the piece of twine until the bow collapsed. He laid it on the mantel, then returned his attention to the package. Turning it over, he eased one edge of the paper open until a tiny patch of knitted fabric became visible.

"Oh, for heaven's sake!" Molly huffed impatiently and threw her hands in the air.

"What?" he asked innocently, then laughed. He loved driving her crazy like that.

Ripping off the rest of the paper, he was left holding…something. Two somethings, in fact. Taking each by the edge, he held them up and studied them before understanding dawned. A quick glance at Molly's beaming face confirmed his suspicion.

Booties!

"Are you sure?"

She laughed. "I'm a midwife, Easton, and my best friend is a doctor. Yes, I'm sure."

Easton swept her up and spun her around the room, their laughter filling the cabin, as it would for years to come. He finally set her down, but he didn't let her go. He would *never* let her go.

"Ready?" she asked, grinning up at him.

Easton sighed, the spell broken, though nothing could ruin this day for him. "Ready as I'll ever be."

They walked hand-in-hand, Easton holding her tight on the icy patches, and arrived at the Institute to find a handful of people already gathered. Stella James, the town midwife, approached them.

"Molly, Commander, Merry Christmas," the old

woman said, holding on to her own husband's arm tightly to maintain her balance. "I wouldn't bother about this today, but it somehow seems like the perfect day for it."

Molly and Easton gave each other puzzled glances.

"What is it?" Easton asked.

"Well, I'm not getting any younger, as you may have noticed, and this winter air sets my arthritis barking louder than a pack of huskies. Rupert here thinks it's time we go live with our son in Florida, now that Molly's here."

Molly frowned. "What do you mean?"

Stella took Molly's hand in her gnarled one and smiled. "The women in this town are like my own children to me. Every time Rupert brought up leaving for a warmer climate, I refused. I wasn't about to subject these ladies to the care of that horrible Dr. Jenkins! But now that you and Dr. Montgomery are here, I feel like I'm leaving the townswomen in very capable hands."

"You mean..." Molly gaped at the woman, then tried again. "You mean you're leaving me your business?"

"If you'll take it on," Stella said. "These ladies need a dedicated midwife like you."

Molly pulled Stella into a fierce hug. Easton had always been a little envious of the way women could communicate with a mere touch. Now that he had Molly, he was learning the language, but he still had a long way to go.

"Let's get this show on the road!" Matthew called out. "It's colder than Rocky the Reindeer's rump out here!"

He and Sinead, Nathaniel and Claire, and Samuel and Beth stood off to one side, all smiling broadly as Easton left Molly and mounted the steps to the Institute's main landing. Turning to face the crowd, he slipped his hand in his pocket and squeezed the tiny knitted booties tucked inside. A sense of profound peace washed over him.

Easton had never thought he'd one day have a family of his own. He wouldn't lie and pretend the idea of fatherhood didn't worry him, but he trusted Molly and his own instincts to show him the way. His first act as a father-to-be would be to send a letter to his superior, accepting the offer to make this position permanent.

Easton had served as a proud member of the Royal North West Mounted Police for more than a decade. Having traveled east to west and back again — more than once — he'd always considered his entire country 'home', but as he looked around Cougar Springs, and the people who lived there, he realized he'd been wrong all along.

This is my home, he thought, *and this is where we will raise our family.*

But now was the time to accept his punishment for having a search party rescue him during the snowstorm. As he had every morning since that day, Easton straightened his back, took a deep lungful of air and started singing. Only this day was different. Instead of fighting butterflies in his stomach as he sang off-key and stumbled over the words, he belted it out with all the pride he held in his heart for his country, his friends and his wife.

"O Canada! Our home and native land! True patriot love in all thy sons command."

Molly mounted the steps, slipped her hand into his free one, and started singing too. Easton had never heard her sing before, and wasn't surprised in the slightest to hear the crisp, sweet soprano of her voice.

"With glowing hearts we see thee rise, the True North strong and free!"

As they sang together, more people gathered around, enjoying the brisk Christmas morning. A few even joined in.

"From far and wide, O Canada, we stand on guard for thee. God keep our land glorious and free!"

By then the entire crowd had joined in, a few singing along in French.

"O Canada, we stand on guard for thee. O Canada, we stand on guard for thee."

After the last long note died, the crowd erupted in cheers and applause, folks hugging each other or shaking hands. Easton's heart nearly burst from his chest with love for his community. It had been there all along, it just took the love of a good woman — the *best* woman — to help him see it.

Squeezing Molly's fingers, he smiled down at her. "Merry Christmas, my love."

Molly returned his smile, clasping his hand in both of hers. "The merriest. The absolute merriest."

And it was.

ALSO BY CASSIE HAYES

MAIL ORDER MOUNTIES
Bride for Nolan
Bride for Dermot
Bride for Easton

GOLD RUSH BRIDES
The Beginning
Emmy

THE DALTON BRIDES
The Drifter's Mail Order Bride
Hank's Rescued Bride
The Marshal's Rebellious Bride

SILVER SPRINGS
Rocky Mountain Hero
Rocky Mountain Home

STANDALONES
Poppy: Bride of Alaska
(American Mail Order Brides)

Hope on the Horizon
(Debra Holland's Montana Sky Kindle World)

Back Home Again (Yosemite Flats)

ABOUT THE AUTHOR

Cassie Hayes grew up pretending she was Laura Ingalls (before that pesky Almonzo arrived on the scene) in the middle of Oregon farm country. She lives with her husband and cat on the Pacific Ocean, and loves to hear from her readers.

Connect with her at:

www.CassieHayes.com
cassie@cassiehayes.com

Made in the USA
Middletown, DE
12 January 2021